DIRTY LITTLE SECRET

A BILLIONAIRE ROMANCE

MIKA LANE

HEADLANDS PUBLISHING

GET A FREE SHORT STORY!

Get a FREE steamy short story!
Join my Insider Group

Enjoy exclusive access to private release specials, giveaways, the opportunity to receive advance reader copies (ARCs), and other random musings.

LET'S KEEP IN TOUCH
Mika Lane Newsletter
Email me
Visit me! www.mikalane.com
Friend me! Facebook
Pin me! Pinterest
Follow me! Twitter
Laugh with me! Instagram

Join Mika's Insider Group
www.mikalane.com
Contact Mika

Copyright© 2020 by Mika Lane
Headlands Publishing
4200 Park Blvd. #244
Oakland, CA 94602

ISBN ebook 978-1-948369-42-8

CHAPTER 1

VARDEN

Thump.

The door slammed, echoing through the building and all the way down the street. All heads turned in my direction.

Just as I'd wanted.

I stood in the entrance, my eyes adjusting to the dim light. This gave me the chance to adjust the Venetian-style mask I'd tugged over my face in the last minutes before entering. It lent me an eerie, and I hoped mysterious, air, and running my fingers over the smooth alabaster and swirly filigree trim was a familiar comfort.

My adjustments served another purpose—they gave me a moment to scope out the room and assess the evening's talent. A head start on the night's possibilities would allow me to decide ahead of time which of the babes in attendance I was gonna spin on my dick before the night was over.

The blue balls that had been killing me weren't letting me forget my mission.

Why the mask? Well, it wasn't for style. I could give a crap about looking like I was a refugee from *Carnivale*. No. Simply put, it was a disguise. No one, and I mean *no one*, in the club knew who I was. And I planned to keep it that way.

The twelve hours a day I worked my hedge fund firm were not exactly relaxing. But the few hours a night I spent at the most secret sex club in San Francisco allowed me to be a different person, something I craved the way a man needs air. At Club Silk I had no responsibility, no fortune, and no celebrity as San Francisco's *wunderkind* financial brain. I didn't even have a goddamn name.

For a few miraculous moments, I, Varden Gallagher didn't exist. And it was fucking amazing.

"G," a female voice dripping with sex purred over my shoulder. Without turning, I knew who it was.

But of course I turned. It would have been rude, and possibly self-desctructive, not to.

"Miss M. Don't you look beautiful tonight."

And she did. The proprietor of Club Silk stood before me in a slamming red evening gown that reminded me of something from the old-time movies my mother had loved. M looked like a movie star and moved like one too.

"Darling." She planted a kiss on the cheek of my mask, no doubt leaving a deep red lipstick mark.

"How are you this evening, G?" she asked.

The first time each night I was called my "club name" was usually jarring. But in a good way. Along with the ritual of pulling on my mask, it was strangely comforting and pushed me into my temporary identity.

I thought of it as a clean transition from the real world to my fantasy one.

I ran a thumb along her cheek, grabbing a strand of her black hair and giving it a tug.

"Oh," she moaned. "If you keep that up, I may have to spirit you away to one of our private rooms."

She'd like that. I, however, would not.

"I could never do that to you. I respect you far too much," I fibbed.

She responded by belting out the laugh of a woman who *owned* the world.

"And why couldn't you do that to me, my dear G?"

I ran a finger down the front of her dress to where it just stopped short of exposing her small but perfect breasts. When I knew I had her, I pushed the silky fabric down, baring a beautiful, dark nipple.

My fingers closed on it and squeezed.

Miss M neither moved, nor altered her expression.

"M," I explained, "because you'd never find satisfaction with another man after me. I couldn't ruin you like that."

How was that for a dick answer?

Her head fell back and she released another beautiful laugh. She smacked my hand right off her tit, tucked herself back into her dress, and whispered, "You can ruin me any day."

With a wink, she floated across the room to greet another guest.

Maybe I *should* fuck her some day.

But like the saying went, you gotta keep your dick out of the company inkwell.

Of course, Silk wasn't my company, per se, but it was my home away from home. I wasn't about to risk any drama with the one person who could keep me away from it.

I'd seen M on the warpath before, and rain down her wrath on some dumb fuck who didn't mind his place.

Regardless, my stiffening cock seemed to like the idea of Miss M, and I reached down to adjust myself in my custom-made trousers.

The industrial space that housed Silk was the perfect venue for an erotic as hell sex club. I'd been to several in my day, and none came close to this one.

Some smart real estate investor—with foresight not even I had had—transformed an old, trashed commercial space, one of the few still standing from San Francisco's days as a huge food cannery, into a giant adult playground.

The city's food processing industry had been driven out long before, and the once industrial part of town was now ground zero for movers and shakers of the tech and financial world, bringing wealth to San Francisco unlike anyone had ever dreamed of.

So this old space, with its abundance of character, had been reconfigured as the dreamy Club Silk, with its warren of bars, dance floors, stages, and play rooms for fucking or whatever else anyone felt like doing.

Miss M had wisely purchased it and taken it to the next level by covering the wall in dark tapestries, and providing just enough light to leave the place candlelit dim, and massively sexy.

But her biggest coup was in making it exclusive *and* keeping it under the radar.

Most San Franciscans had heard of the place but weren't sure whether it truly existed, or whether it was just another urban myth. A lucky few of us knew where the truth lie, and we paid handsomely for the privilege. This kept out the riff-raff, the creepy guys who walked around with their dicks in their hands, and kept the gorgeous women coming in.

And it all gave me an escape I'd die without.

A female hand landed on my arm.

"Hey."

I turned to see the voluptuous redhead I'd fucked a couple weeks ago.

"How are you?" I asked. Too bad I was in the mood for a spinner tonight, because this woman was fucking hot. Her curvy ass might be worth revisiting, though, depending on how the night progressed.

"I thought you were gonna call me," she said with a delicious pout. My cock jerked again as I remembered her lips wrapped around my hard wood.

"A." I think that was her club name. It was hard to keep all the goddamn initials straight. "You know I never call. It's just not my thing."

Her gaze drilled into my eyes, the only part of my face she could see behind the mask. I know she wanted to see more. They always did.

She, too, wore a mask, but it covered only the upper half of her face, which allowed me to enjoy her pretty smile. Her red lips were always ready for whatever she got the urge to do, and lucky for me that had included sucking me off to a point where I'd nearly lost consciousness.

A true cocksucker she was, and I meant that in the nicest possible way.

But I didn't normally repeat women. That was the beauty of Silk.

In consolation, I ran my thumb along her lower lip and dipped it into her willing mouth.

The old cock shifted again, reminding me to get on with the female attention I so desperately needed, and to stop being so goddamn coy. I retrieved my thumb. Time to get back to assessing other, new talent.

"See you later, hon," I said, heading for the building's massive second floor, a mezzanine with a perfect view of everything below.

The elevator, a rickety old freight thing, was moving at its usual glacial speed. But I kept pressing the *up* button anyway, as if that would make a difference. Probably someone in there playing out their elevator fucking fantasy. I had to shake my head and chuckle. I'd tried that when I was a newbie at the club, too.

As a noob, I'd wanted to fuck in every nook and cranny of the place, and the more people who could see and watch me, the better. Of course, this was always done with my mask in place.

Most clubgoers wore some version of one, as well. Those of us with a lot to lose guarded our privacy to a point bordering on obsession.

You couldn't be too careful, as the saying went.

But these days I preferred playing with some sweet female in the smaller rooms, and even on occasion in one of the private rooms with locking doors.

As much as I dug being watched, getting off was the top priority now that I was a seasoned club member. I no longer craved the ego boost of being watched like I once did—it actually made it damn hard to come, truth be told.

No, filling some hot thing's pussy, mouth, or ass with my big load was my kryptonite.

I bailed on the slow elevator and headed for the stairs. In keeping with the rest of the building, they were a wide, creaky contraption barely sturdy enough to pass city inspection, not to mention support the couple going at it doggy style on the second step. As I climbed past them, I nodded at the dude. He was drilling a screaming woman with her dress pushed up to her tits and her pretty ass up in the air, and he didn't miss a beat. He nodded right back while he held her arms behind her back.

Nice.

Up on the mezzanine, I found three beauties in various stages of undress—mostly completely undressed, actually—cuddling on a large velvet sofa, sipping champagne from tall flutes they held with perfectly manicured fingers.

I made a quick mental calculation of which I liked best, and which I would settle for, if need be. Not to be a dick about it—I loved fucking all women. I just knew what I needed that night, and if I could find it, well *bingo*.

"Ladies." I nodded at them. Lord, they were cute.

"Hey, take that mask off. I wanna see your face," the voluptuous one demanded.

"Sorry, babe. No can do."

They scooted a place open for me on the sofa and the blonde one patted a spot next to her. "Have a seat, masked man."

I squeezed between the hips of two of the beauties. Christ, they were all stunners.

"I've seen you here before. I know that mask," the skinny brunette said. "What's your name?"

"G. What are yours?"

"X."

"Y."

"And—"

"Don't tell me," I interrupted. I pointed at the brunette. "Your name is Z."

She shrugged with a lovely laugh. "Somebody knows his alphabet. We got a smart one here, ladies"

If she only knew.

I smiled under my mask, not that they could see it. Damn thing was making me hot, one of the hazards of wearing it.

I removed my suit jacket and roll up the sleeves of my starched, cotton shirt to cover the initials on my cuff: *VG.* They knew the G. They didn't need to know the V.

"You're funny, Miss Z. Why don't you do a little dance for me?"

"Yeah, Z," X said. "Show us your stuff."

"I can do that." She stood, taking a position in front of us, and commenced to gyrating, wearing only fuck me high heels and a lacy thong panty.

My dick strained against my trousers, the compression approaching downright pain.

8

"You're fucking beautiful, Z, you know that?"

I reached to place my hands on her lovely hips, but she stepped back, just beyond my reach.

Fair enough.

I stood. "I'll be in the playroom on the third floor. Just letting you know."

I left them in a flurry of protests and headed for the best part of the club, the one place in the universe to truly scratch my itch.

CHAPTER 2

SAFFI

"Yo, Saff."

I loved Tom's nickname for me. Actually, I loved a lot of things about him.

If he only knew.

"Hey, how's your day going?" I poked my head in his office door. Was he going to ask me to lunch? *Finally?* Or insist I join him in co-authoring a piece he was doing for the newspaper, which would be sure to win us both a Pulitzer prize.

"Saff, on your way back to your cube, would you mind running this stuff down to the mailroom for me?"

What. The. Fuck.

Without waiting for an answer, he turned back to his computer where he was most likely working on that Pulitzer prize winner, *without me.*

"Finally got my damn bills paid," he muttered to himself. He reached for the ringing phone on his desk.

"San Francisco Post. Tom here."

I lumbered down to the dark and foul depths of our newspaper building to drop off Tom's bills, without a thank you I might add, and slunk back to my own hole of a cubicle. I'd been assigned a remote location on my first day there a few months before, conveniently stuck between the kitchen and the restrooms.

I had the pleasure of enjoying my coworkers' smelly lunches and flushing toilets. All day long.

But even a shitty cube location in office Siberia was not without its perks. No one happened by unless they had a reason to, and I could always hear them coming. It was lonely, but gave me plenty of opportunity to read things like *How to Get the Career You want, Do Nice Girls Finish Last?*, and *You Don't Get What You Don't Ask For*.

And to look at the shoes on Zappos, of course.

In fact, just that morning I'd read an article about "taking the bull by the horns" and "making it happen," right before I'd dribbled coffee down the front of my white blouse.

Like it was that easy.

I was the office bitch, no doubt. I got the bottom of the barrel assignments, had to run for Chinese food every day, and made all the trips to the nasty mailroom. What if I came up with a challenging assignment on my own, rather than waiting to be given one? And what if I dazzled everyone with a great job?

I could see it now. A new cube, far away from the

kitchen and toilets. Maybe even an office. With a window, of course. But I wasn't greedy. A little spot where I could see even a slice of sky would be perfectly acceptable…

And then, imagine not having to be the Chinese food/mail room gopher. No, I'd suggest something more fair like having people take turns running for the food. Or even better—paying the extra ten bucks and having the food *delivered*. Imagine.

But for now, I had to get back to my shitty little assignments covering Little League and the Garden Club.

The day crept by. I'd managed a first draft of both my lame story assignments, leaving plenty of time for perusing career websites and my favorite dating blog, *Getting that Guy to Notice You*.

Just setting the damn world on fire…yup, that's me.

Because my cube was off the beaten path, if I wanted to join the gang for after work drinks, I had to listen for when they were heading out. I'd been forgotten on more than one occasion. But instead of feeling sorry for myself, I'd just joined the party as if they couldn't possibly have a good time without me. Bright smiles and witticisms all around. They were gonna love me if it killed them. Or me.

And today was like no other. There was a rustle of backpacks, coats, and purses filtering through the air—a sure signal to catch up with the group and casually blend in.

"Hey guys," I said, hoisting my backpack on one shoulder.

"Saffi!" the editor in chief said. "Glad you're joining us. This will be fun."

"Never miss it!" I said.

You jerks are not leaving my ass behind. Not today, anyway.

My coworkers crammed into the elevator for the ride down. There really wasn't room for me, but I laughed and pushed inside anyway, stepping on several toes, and pretending not to notice. Then I tagged after them to the divey Irish bar not far from the office.

The place blared sporting events from around the world—mostly soccer—on TV screens hanging from every corner. The furniture consisted of rough, splintery picnic tables covered in graffiti carvings. You had to be careful what you touched. At least, I did. But the place had ninety-nine cent happy hour beers, which suited my budget just fine.

After all, I still freaking lived at home, and there was no end in sight to that. I'd have to make three times as much money as I currently did just to afford a crappy room in a crappy group house in a crappy San Francisco neighborhood before I could even think of moving out of my dad's house.

Everyone grabbed a seat, leaving me on the end, which was not so bad really because it was next to Tom. The noise in the bar made it difficult if not impossible to hear the banter, but I pretended to understand and was sure to burst out laughing when everyone else did. A second and then a third round of cheap beer was served, and I pushed closer to hear the conversation, no longer much worried about office decorum.

Beer did that to me.

My boobs brushed against Tom's arm, but I was feeling a bit slutty and didn't care. He ordered me another beer, and then another beer, gentleman that he was. The plight of my life faded into the background, and it wasn't long before the group thinned out by ones and twos— folks needing to get home to make dinner, pick kids up from soccer, that sort of thing.

A hand landed on my thigh, and I looked around, realizing Tom and I were the only ones left.

He turned to me. "I gotta go soon, too. What about you?"

I flipped my hair. "Oh yeah. I have tons of things I need to do, too," I said, looking at my watch for emphasis. Except I'd forgotten to wear it.

I reached for my wallet, but Tom took my hand. God that felt nice. Maybe today was the day he'd see me as something other than the office newbie.

"Don't worry about the bill," he said with a smile. "The boss got it. I mean, it's the least she could do when beers are only freaking ninety-nine cents. Don't you think?" He rolled his eyes.

"Oh yes, absolutely. I just wasn't sure she remembered before she left."

"What were you going to do if she had? Foot the bill? On your measly salary?" He laughed, shaking his head.

Heat ran up and over my face. "Well, if she hadn't paid it, one of us would have had to," I said.

He slammed the last of his beer, set it down, and wiped his mouth with the back of his hand.

"Um, no," he said with a furtive glance around. "I'd just

leave. They're so busy here, they wouldn't know for hours."

What?

"You'd just walk out on the bill?"

He looked like I'd told him the Earth was flat. "Well, you don't have to put it like that. I mean, it's not something I'd do anywhere else besides this dump."

"Anyhoo." He slid closer and put his hand on my thigh. "Have I told you how cute you are, Saff?"

A warning stirred over me, however weak. My bullshit detector was severely weakened if not outright disabled by the beer.

It wasn't completely out of order, though.

"Thanks," I said, looking down at his hand, which had just made itself home even further up my thigh. As I tried to figure out what to do with this unfounded affection, he smashed his lips against mine. I yanked my head back in reflex.

He leaned closer. "C'mon Saff. You can't deny there's an attraction between us."

Okay. Yeah, I wanted to kiss him. But in a freaking dive bar after five beers? When there could be coworkers lurking around.

What if someone came back for a forgotten jacket or backpack?

"Um. I don't know, Tom. I think I'd better head out. Gotta catch my bus." I stumbled as I stood, whacking my knee while extricating myself from the picnic bench. He stood, too.

"Shit," I said.

"Hey, careful there," he said, making no effort to help

me catch my balance. Nor did he wait for me before heading to the door.

I hustled to catch up. Yeah, I was that stupid.

"Well, beautiful," he said, turning to me out on the sidewalk. "Guess I'll see ya tomorrow. Maybe you can help me with fact-checking that big profile piece I'm doing on the mayor. That would be fun for you, right?"

Ugh. Fact checking. Shit job of all shit jobs.

"Yeah, sure, Tom." I looked up the street and saw my bus coming. I could make it if I ran. "I gotta—"

But before I could get the words out, his lips pressed against mine once again. This time I kissed him back, letting his tongue tease my lips and explore my mouth. If he hadn't reeked of beer, he might actually have smelled good. But his hand on my breast snapped me out of my trance.

"Hey..." I said.

"Well sweetie," he replied, unfazed, zipping his jacket. "See ya tomorrow." He smiled and strode off, as if he kissed his colleagues all the time. Maybe he did.

Like a dipshit, I stood there on the curb as Tom disappeared around the corner.

The bus!

I turned to sprint for it, but was too late. Half a block away, its doors slammed shut, and it drew away from the curb, engines gunning in preparation for the climb up the steep San Francisco street that lay ahead. Figured.

There wouldn't be another bus for twenty minutes, so I got comfortable in a urine-scented bus shelter and watched the traffic go by. The evening wind was picking up and the fog blowing in, which sent all kinds of flotsam and jetsum blustering through the street. Included in the frenzy was a torn business card, which wedged itself under a corner of my shoe.

I wouldn't normally touch street garbage, but the word "erotic" caught my eye. Erotic *what?*

I picked up the tattered paper using my fingernails.

> Club Silk
> San Francisco's most exclusive, erotic—

But the rest was torn off. All that was left was a barely-readable phone number. And the card must have been old, because it was missing the area code now required of all phone calls.

Club Silk? What the hell was that?

CHAPTER 3

VARDEN

I parked my Audi RS7 in the Union Square parking garage and darted through the morning rush hour traffic to meet my tailor, Ivan. I was in a shit mood, bent about how things had gone down the night before at the club.

The prior evening, after having left the alphabet ladies X, Y, and Z, I'd headed up to the club's third floor, to a nondescript door bearing the sign, *Twist Room*. With a quiet knock, a little window slid aside, followed by the door opening and closing as I ducked inside.

Ahhh, heaven.

"Yo, G," said a huge bald guy, one of the club's bouncers. He grabbed my hand and pulled me into that half shake, half hug thing guys do. He was of an impressive size, making even me look short. His head was shiny and smooth, he wore thick hoop earrings, and he had tattoos on his neck that disappeared into his shirt collar.

"How've you been, my friend?" I asked.

"I'm all right. Looking forward to getting a pussy later on tonight," he said.

I nodded. "You and me both."

I slapped him on the back and made my way into a room covered in yards of rich velvet, smelling vaguely of sex and expensive perfume, thumping with the deep bass of house music.

Silk tufted mattresses lined the room's borders. It was early yet, so there wasn't much to watch except for a few eager couples, so I settled into a plushy couch where I'd have the perfect viewpoint when things did heat up. In time, the room would be packed to the point where the bouncer would be forced to turn people away.

He'd would never turn me away, though.

Without asking, a server floated by and placed a Maker's Mark in my hand. *This* was what privilege bought. Such were the benefits of access to the most exclusive room in the most exclusive club; they knew my name—well, club name—and they knew my drink. Only members were permitted into the Twist Room.

Unless of course a beautiful woman wanted in. The door opened for them without hesitation.

As it should.

I pushed my mask up just enough to take a couple sips of bourbon and a near-instant warmth washed over me. My days as a hedge fund manager were getting more and more stressful with the ups and downs of the financial markets, not to mention nervous clients, and Club Silk was just what the doctor ordered.

If doctors ordered sex clubs.

I'd positioned myself in view of of a tufted bed where, right in front of me, a woman with her dress pulled up to her waist straddled the face of the man beneath her. It was clear from the motion of her grinding hips that the guy's tongue was buried in her pussy, his hands reaching up to knead her hanging breasts. After a few minutes of obliterating the guy's face —I didn't know how he was managing to breath—her head began to buck.

Damn, watching a woman come was hot.

I unzipped my pants to reach through a tangle of shirttails and boxers. When my cramped cock was finally free, I stroked it in rhythm to the woman's movements. Her moaning increased, and the man took hold of her nipples, twisting them without mercy.

This last effort sent her over the edge. She moaned and screamed like a banshee until the guy eating her lifted her from his face, flipped her over, and drove his cock deep inside her. The others in the room stopped to watch as the man pounded her pussy so hard she nearly flew off the mattress. More than one male observer had his cock in his hand.

The Twist Room's door blew open for a second, and I looked up as my dancer, Z, entered, holding a just-refilled champagne flute. She paused to scan the room, and those in attendance looked back in admiration at her high-heeled nakedness.

Somehow, between the minutes when I last saw her, and now, her thong panty had disappeared. Her smooth, tan hips and juicy tits made my dick even harder, and I had to focus to keep from exploding. When she finally saw me, she headed over, jiggling ever so slightly thanks to the champagne and high heels.

"Hey there," she said, looking down at me, dick in hand.

Her flawless skin glistened, most likely thanks to expensive oils and lotions. Her pussy was clean of hair save for a small patch just above her slit. That seemed to be the style of the day—called a *landing strip* or something like that. I didn't care what they called it as long as the little patch led right to the goods.

She posed right in front of me, so close I could inhale the scent of her sweet, girl-next-door pussy. Just the way I liked it.

"Hey." I leaned back in my chair, jiggling the ice cubes in my bourbon. "You wanna come closer?"

She obliged, wedging herself between my knees until her navel was inches from my nose. Damn, her skin was smooth.

"I want to see more. Show me your pussy," I growled, hand still on my cock.

She lifted one high-heeled foot onto the arm of the sofa, opening herself wide enough to show me the plump lips and hard clit leading to her glistening opening.

"May I?" I leaned toward her.

She nodded with a sly smile and I set my drink aside. My fingers wandered to the very top of her lips and explored the groove leading to her cute little clit. I ran my finger up and down, spreading her juices, while she ground into my hand. Slipping one finger inside her, I made a "come here" motion to get at her G spot. When she ground against my hand, I slipped in another.

Hers was one tight pussy, which I wouldn't have minded tasting if not for my mask.

"That feels nice," she murmured, eyes narrowed, lips parted. She clawed at my hair for balance, and her own head lolled back.

I removed my fingers and wrapped my hands around her ass, lifting her up as I rose from my seat. With her legs wrapped around me, I brought her to one of the tufted mattresses and laid her down.

"Fuck me," she whispered

"Yeah, Miss Z? You want my cock?" I fished through my pocket for a condom.

"Please. Please."

I stretched the rubber over my erection, and she spread her legs like a freaking contortionist. She grabbed me like a hungry animal, pulling me toward her opening. I paused to make sure she was ready, and in one quick movement, she bucked her hips and engulfed my entire dick.

A small audience formed around us, making my cock even harder. If that were possible.

I leaned over her and said through my mask, "You feel so good. Damn."

"Your cock is wonderful, baby. Give it to me. I'm gonna come quick."

I plunged into her up to my balls, and she gave a shriek, her head banging against the mattress, her hands grabbing my ass to pull me closer.

Her breath came fast and hard in my ear. "Fuck me, please. Yes, just like that."

Her pussy pulsed, gripping my cock, and my balls

tightened as my own explosion drew nearer. I kept pumping her as she came again…and again.

I fucked her until she couldn't speak. Sweat poured down my face, puddling inside my mask, tickling my nose. I was getting close to exhaustion, ready for my own damn orgasm.

So I kept pumping. Z had gone nearly comatose, her head rocking back and forth, small whimpers escaping her lips.

Fuck.

I knew it.

I wasn't gonna come.

God fucking dammit.

I pulled out, pissed as hell. Z, in her state, seemed not to even notice. I yanked off my rubber and sat for a moment on the edge of the mattress, pants around my ankles, cock hard as a baseball bat, balls aching, while the crowd dispersed, unaware of my frustration.

Z sat up next to me. She looked like she'd just finished a marathon.

"You okay?" she asked, placing a hand on my arm.

"Yeah, sweetie. You're incredible."

I stood, pulling my pants up, tucking everything back in. "I gotta run, babe. I'll see ya."

She smiled and waved weakly.

I marched past the bouncer and out the door, moving as fast as my aching balls would let me.

Downstairs I brushed by Miss M, who called after me.

"G! Will I see you again soon—"

But I just kept going. Blue balls did that to me. Halfway down the block I remembered to remove my mask, and when I did, cool evening air washed over my sweaty face.

If I couldn't get off at the club, there would always be another time. But for now, there was home, with a little help from my friend, internet porn.

CHAPTER 4

SAFFI

I entered my boss's office—the editor in charge of city news—and closed the door. I was about to lay a bomb on him, which had the potential to change my life. Well, that was the idea, anyway.

He waved me to the chair opposite his desk, continuing to tap on his keyboard.

"Done in a sec, Saffi," he said.

I cooled my heels patiently, looking around at the framed articles and awards covering the walls. "Ed, is this a good time? Because I can come back."

"What? No, it's great." He hit *send* on his computer, took off his glasses, and turned to me. "You have my full attention now. Sorry about that. My mother's going into a home, and I had to get some insurance information to the administrator there."

Now I felt like a shithead. "Oh, gosh. I didn't know that. I'm sorry."

He waved away her concerns. "It's for the best. We should have done it ages ago."

He folded his hands on his desk and looked at me expectantly.

I took a deep breath. "Okay then. I wanted to pitch you a story idea. It's completely different from anything I've done here. In fact, it's pretty different from anything the City Desk has done."

Ed sat back in his chair. "Really? You've got me intrigued."

"It's a bit of a sensitive topic, but I'm going to speak frankly if you don't mind."

A dribble of sweat ran down the back of my neck.

"You can always be straight with me, Saffi. We're a news organization. We've seen it all."

Well, he might not have seen this one...

"Ed, have you ever heard of Club Silk?"

His brows knit. "Yeah, I have. That sex club, right? We looked into it a couple years back and couldn't determine whether or not it really existed. Couldn't get any leads, so we dropped it. Concluded it was an urban myth."

Maybe I *was* gonna be the office hero, after all.

"It *does* exist Ed. And I want to do a story on it."

His mouth opened. Then it closed.

"Are are you sure? We determined there was no such place. And even if there were, wouldn't you want to give the story to a more senior member of the staff—"

Yeah. Um, fuck no.

I cut him off. "I can do it. I want to do it. I want to prove myself, show you I can do reporting beyond Little League and Garden Clubs."

That didn't sound too complain-y, did it?

He studied me, no doubt looking at me in a new light. One of a professional, confident, and talented woman.

"I really think this ought to be assigned to—"

No fucking way.

I smiled sweetly. "*I* got the lead. And I'm not passing it on. I'm just not." I gripped my hands until they started to go numb.

He wasn't convinced. Yet. "You know that's not how we operate here. We have the most qualified staff member cover each story."

I leaned toward him, balls out. "This is gold. And it's *my* gold. You have to let me do it. This is the chance of a lifetime."

Shit, did I just say that?

He stared at me, apparently as surprised as I was by my newfound brazenness. "Tell me about your approach."

"I'm ninety-nine percent sure I have an in. I want to go undercover as a guest of the club and see what it's all about."

"Are you sure? You want to go to a *sex* club?" he asked with incredulity.

Jesus, did he think I was a fucking virgin?

A burning heat crept across my face, like it always did when I was stressed. But this was more from excitement than embarrassment. The words *sex club* made my heart pound. I squeezed my knees together to head off the growing throb. But it only intensified.

"Yeah, Ed. I do want to go. So that I can do my story."

He leaned back and stared at the ceiling. With a deep

inhale, he said, "Shit, Saffi. What if something happens to you?"

"It's a *sex* club, not a murder club. What's the worst that could happen?"

This time, it was Ed's turn to blush.

"I...I mean. Whatever. You know what I mean." He began to nod, very slowly. "I don't know. Maybe we could give it a try. You think you can get in?"

Score. I had him.

"Almost positive. Besides, if not, there's no story."

He chuckled. "I have a hard time imagining you writing about sex."

Things you hope your boss never says to you.

"But it's a good idea. It could be a very, very interesting story," he added.

A knock rattled the door behind me and Ed glanced at the wall clock. "Let's keep this confidential for a few days. I want to make sure you can kick it off." He motioned behind me for his next meeting to come in.

"Hey, Saff," Tom said.

Mr. *Dine 'n Dash.*

"Hey." I brushed by him and turned to Ed at the last minute. "Thanks, Ed. I really appreciate it."

"Yup," he said, and turned his attention to Tom.

I ran back to my desk needing the privacy of my cube to jump up and down and scream with silent happiness. What luck. First, I found that business card at the bus stop after sucking face with Tom, who turned out to be not as cool as I'd thought.

Then, I'd gotten Ed's approval to at least start the story. Going in, I'd figured my chances were only about fifty-fifty. But I won. I was finally going to get the respect I deserved. Not to mention entrance to a sex club.

Hot and bothered by not only my my first victory, but also the prospect of going to a sex club, I scurried to the ladies room at the far end of the building, the one no one ever used but me.

Locked in a stall, I inched my skirt up and panties down, closing my eyes, trying to picture what such a club might be like.

And, of course, what shoes I might wear.

I actually had no freaking idea, but I made a mental note to check Google. There was always something to be found online. But until I did, *not* knowing made it all the more fun to imagine.

Leaning on the wall, I ran my fingers up and down my soaking slit, spreading the wetness up my lips to my hard clit. With a few strokes, I began to shudder, and went to town until I exploded in a silent orgasm, catching myself on the stall door before my knees buckled and I wiped out on the floor. Not glamorous, but it did the job.

Until recently, I always pictured Tom when I played with myself, but I was done with that douchebag. Now, it was time for something new.

CHAPTER 5

VARDEN

I arrived at my tailor's shop, a place easily and often underestimated. The entrance was nothing more than an old storefront door that said *pull*. No sign, no indication that two floors up existed the most talented and sought-after custom suit maker in San Francisco.

My city was ground zero for "business casual," which meant I didn't need many suits. But I wanted to make sure that *my* version of business casual was more considered than the khaki Dockers and white, button-down Oxford shirts everyone else wore that they'd picked up at Macy's. I'd come a long way from my childhood of hand-me-downs and the occasional splurge at Sears.

Ivan, the proprietor, ran to greet me with a handshake and slap on the back.

"Well if it isn't Varden Gallagher! Good to see you, my man. You've been well, I trust?" He was short and stocky, with an exotic-sounding Eastern European lastname. I had no idea where he was from; he'd always avoided answering the question.

"Hey Ivan. Great to see you, too." I scanned the shop for something that might work for a new trousers or a sports jacket. Across the room, Ivan's assistant, a big-titted blonde who loved to suck cock in the privacy of the dressing room, waved.

"Hello, Mr. Gallagher," Olga cooed from across the room. "I saw your name on the schedule for this morning."

Indeed.

Sounded like she might be game for a little fun...especially if Ivan ran out for a smoke like he frequently did.

He brought over several bolts of fabric.

"These cottons, my friend, are the finest I've seen in my long career. I recommend for you half a dozen new shirts made from it. I can get them to you in two week's time."

I fingered the fabrics. It was nice, but felt like every other shirt hanging in my closet.

Oh, what the hell.

"Six new shirts would be great. I trust you to take good care of me with your recommendations."

Ivan clapped his hands. "I love working with you, Varden. You are a man of distinction. Good taste and classy. I wish every client was like you."

He turned to his associate. "Olga, my dear, please take Mr. Gallagher into the dressing room for a new set of measurements. We want to make sure our records are up-to-date."

Well. I was going to get my early morning blowie, after

all. Six shirts and a cocksucker. What more could a guy want?

"Varden, my friend, please excuse me. I need to step out to address a very disgusting habit. Olga will take good care of you, just as she always does." He reached for a handshake. "Thank you, my friend. I'll have the shirts delivered to your office."

And with that, he grabbed his smokes and split.

Olga was on me before Ivan was even down the stairs, carrying a notebook as if she were really going to re-take the measurements they'd had on file for me for years. Which hadn't changed a bit.

She led me to the dressing room I'd been in a dozen times before, with mirrors on three sides and a block in the middle to stand on for hemming pants. It came in handy for other things, too. She pointed and I knew to step onto it.

Without a word, she was before me. She was short, and with me on the block, she was directly in front of my crotch.

"C'mon, baby," she said in her scratchy, smoker's voice.

I unbuckled my trousers and let them fall to the floor.

She pushed my shirt tails aside and lowered my boxers. My hard-on nearly slapped her face, and she drew back, chuckling with her throaty laugh. She took my dick, her fingers barely able to encircle it, and licked the precum from the tip.

"Tastes so good," she murmured.

"Yeah?" I glanced back at the dressing room door. "Is the door locked Olga?"

But she couldn't answer. Her mouth had devoured me so deeply my cock banged the back of her throat.

She released me for a moment, gasping for air. "Mr. Gallagher, I love sucking your cock."

Well then. To hell with the door.

She got back to work with her customary enthusiasm. I grew closer to exploding and my balls pulled in tight.

I rocked my hips into her face, watching in the room's floor to ceiling mirrors. I also glanced at my watch. I had a meeting at nine a.m. sharp.

To hurry things along, I grabbled her by the hair and started fucking her face. She finally gagged, her eyes watering thick rivers of black mascara down her face. Her right hand furiously pumped her pussy, and it looked like she might come before me.

She pistoned my cock at breakneck speed.

And kept going.

And going.

Holy shit.

I couldn't come. Again.

I pulled myself from her mouth before she bit me.

The front door tinkled, and Ivan's voice boomed through the shop. "Olga! Are you done with Mr. Gallagher?"

You could say we're done.

I eased myself back into my clothes and pulled up my trousers, leaving Olga in the dressing room to clean herself up.

I ran smack into Ivan as I hustled out the door, my achy balls preventing me from moving as fast as I might have liked to.

"I'll look forward to getting those shirts, Ivan."

~

Back in traffic, I saw I'd missed a couple calls. My admin let me know my first appointment of the day would be late due to a delayed flight. The other voicemail was from Beau, my younger brother.

You never knew what you were going to get with him.

"Var. Dude. Hey, I need a little help with something. I'm kinda broke. Will you call me back?"

Beau sounded drunk, or high, or maybe both. As usual, I would find out what the hell he'd been up to. In the past, it had been gambling debts, or he'd owed drug dealers, or he'd been kicked out of the most recent halfway home where he was staying. Whatever it was, Beau's life was a far cry from mine of custom-made clothing, sex clubs, and blowjobs in dressing rooms.

CHAPTER 6

SAFFI

Despite my awesome day, the bus home that night was as miserable as it usually was—bumpy, slow, overheated, and smelling of too many humans crammed into too small a space. When I squeezed out at my stop, I took a deep breath of the foggy evening to shake off the stink of a city commute.

"Hey, Dad. I'm home," I hollered, once inside.

"In here, sweetie."

Dropping my backpack, I headed for my dad's office, a gorgeous, masculine room lined with books, leather furniture, and a giant desk. And the faint smell of scotch in the air.

"You have a good day?" he asked, his silver head turning. The slight wrinkles around his blue eyes sprang into action as he smiled. He might have been my dad, but I could say with confidence that he was damn handsome.

How much should I tell him about my project? Everything? Nothing? Or just a little?

On second thought, he didn't need to know anything.

"It was pretty good, Dad. How was yours?"

He leaned back in his chair and a swell of love thumped in my chest. The man had raised me single-handedly after my mother had passed. No meeting at his busy law firm was ever more important than one of my softball games or dance recitals.

To me, he was everything that was good about the world.

"Day was good," he said, nodding. "Things are booming at the firm. Knock wood," he said, rapping his knuckles on the desk. His firm was one of the largest in San Francisco, but he took nothing for granted. "How are things at the paper?"

I leaned forward, forearms on thighs, hands clasped. "Well, you know how I've been getting crappy little assignments?"

"Like that Garden Club thing?" he asked.

"Exactly. I have a plan to do more."

His eyebrows rose.

"I got a lead on a club here in town. An exclusive club, one that not many people know about. I may go under-cover and see what I can learn."

Concern washed over his face. "What kind of club? Like a country club?"

Ugh. Time to lie.

I hated lying to my dad.

"Kind of like that. Kind of like an exclusive country club, but it's in the city."

Time to wrap up this conversation. I clapped my hands together and turned to go.

"Wait a minute." His hand made a *stop* sign.

Shit. Of course he had more questions.

"Why do you have to go undercover? Is it unsafe?" His furrowed brow said it all.

I should have kept my big mouth shut.

"Of course it's safe." I laughed nervously. Wasn't it? "It's just that I can get a different story posing as a member. That's all."

"You know, Saffi, you don't have to do this."

"Do what?" Now I was the one frowning.

"Scrape by at the Post. They give you crappy work and crappy pay. I'm happy to have you here in the house, but some day, you'll want a place of your own. Hell, you probably want that now. I could get you a job at the firm, starting as a paralegal, and you could attend law school at night."

He was right. Partially. I could take the path of least resistance. Get a job at Dad's firm. Live the easy life. But that's not what I wanted.

Mom, also a journalist, had never taken the easy route. 'Course, she'd married Dad back when San Francisco wasn't as expensive as it had gotten, so they could afford her low-paying career.

But I wasn't giving up. At least not yet.

"Dad. I know you're speaking out of concern. And I love you for that. But I've got to give this a go."

He threw his hands in the air for effect, but a huge smile spread across his face. "I know you do. You're just like your mother."

All good. Time to escape before he asked more questions. "Thanks. I'm tired. I'm going upstairs to take a bath and read for awhile."

"Okay. And hey. I love you," he said.

I walked over and planted a kiss on his cheek. A lump formed in my throat, and I scooted out of the room.

Fast.

I closed the door to the room I'd had since childhood and leaned back against it. Now was the moment of truth. I dialed the number from the tattered business card.

It rang several times, followed by a long beep.

I proceeded to leave my message. "Um, hello. This is Saff—I mean, this is Susan. I, um, wanted some info about the club."

My statements were coming out like questions. I hated that. I cleared my throat.

"Yes, I'm wanting to come by the club. I'm considering joining. That is, if you're taking new members. I'd appreciate your returning my call."

My phone rang ten minutes later while I was in the tub, nearly asleep in the steamy water. I didn't normally bring my phone when I was bathing, but who knew what a sex club's office hours were?

"Hello?"

"Is this Susan?" an authoritative female voice asked.

Susan? Oh *Susan*.

I straightened up in the tub, splashing water onto the floor.

"Yes. Yes, this is she." Remain calm, remain cool.

"We received a message from you."

That was it? Okay. I could play that game.

"Is this my return call from the Club Silk?" I asked, with equal authority.

"Yes, Susan."

"Super. I'd like to come check it out."

"How did you hear about us, Susan?"

Shoulda known they'd ask that.

"A friend. A friend told me I might like it."

"Who, may I ask?" The caller was polite and yet forceful. Good approach.

"I'm afraid I can't share their name." I pictured the tattered piece of paper blowing up to the bus stop.

"Very well. Are you free tomorrow night?"

Are you kidding?

"Why yes. I am." Shit. What would I wear?

"Do you have a pen?"

I looked around the bathroom. Of course I didn't have a pen. Who had a pen in the bathroom?

"No. Why?"

"You need to know how to get here."

Right. Duh.

"Can you text me the address?"

There was silence on the line. Then a sigh. "Yes. I'll text you the information."

What a gal.

"Thank you."

"What time will we see you?"

"Around nine p.m. okay?"

"Yes, see you then," said the clipped voice.

"By the way, when I get there, who do I ask for—"

Click.

Okay, then. The woman was not going to win any awards for customer service.

I settled back into the tepid water. It was time to get out, before I turned into a prune, but thinking about the club had me excited again. My hand wandered down to my pussy, where I found my clit, hard and erect, for the second time that day.

Mmmm.

I reached farther down to my opening, which had not surprisingly become quite slippery in all the excitement. Another finger joined my first. Initially, I made slow circles around my clit, still sensitive from my session a few hours earlier. My nipples tightened and poked through the surface of the bath, and with my free hand, I pinched and pulled them.

What would the club be like? Dark and dreamy? Would people be fucking right out in the open? Going at it in every nook and cranny? I couldn't wait to find out. Not participate, of course. Just observe. This was strictly work.

I pictured a beautiful woman, legs covered in thigh-high stockings. She bent forward, her ass in the air for all the world to see.

A tall, dark stranger stood behind her, holding his giant erect cock just at the opening to her pussy.

She raised her hips to open herself to him, and he slowly entered. Once he was halfway in, she bucked against him, begging for more. The man pulled her long hair, her back curving into what looked like an uncomfortable arch. But she didn't seem to mind, and in fact bucked harder, releasing a scream that filled the room. All heads turned to see her, and several observers moved closer for a better view.

With his hand full of her hair, the man plunged his cock inside her. Her mouth hung open, her body convulsing. Her hands pulled her ass cheeks open in case there was a possibility he could drive his cock even deeper. He pumped faster and faster, and when he released her hair, her head bounced wildly. A series of guttural cries announced her explosion into an orgasm.

Her lover was not far behind. with another pump, and he threw his head back, releasing a string of profanities...

I'd had been rubbing my clit in time to my imaginary friends, my own orgasm building to a crescendo. I gasped as my climax gripped me, leaving me shaking in the now-cold bath water.

This sex club stuff promising to be both fun *and* career-boosting.

CHAPTER 7

VARDEN

The City Grille was an old San Francisco institution with dark paneling, leather booths, and strong cocktails. I walked past the hostess stand to meet my attorney, for dinner.

"Hugh, good to see you." I clapped him on the back. He was a great guy, and had represented my firm and me for years.

"You, too, Varden. It's been awhile. Where does the time go?"

"I have no idea. It's been a couple months since the last deal you helped us with. Seems like last week."

Hugh waved the waiter over. "What're you drinking? I'm quite happy here with my Maker's Mark."

"Same please," I said to the waiter.

"Hey," Hugh said, "I hope you don't mind, but my daughter may join us at some point. Her office is just around the corner."

"That'd be great."

"She just graduated from college and is working for the newspaper," Hugh explained.

"No kidding. That must be fun."

"Well, I'm not sure how much fun it is. They pay her shit, so she's stuck living at home, at least for the time being." He shook his head.

"Oh, I remember those days," I said. "I don't know what's worse—being broke *in* college or being broke *after* college thanks to your shitty first job."

While we caught up on business, a couple women at the bar made no secret of their interest in us. They had a world-worn look with bleached hair, spray tans, and overly Botoxed foreheads. They weren't really my type, not sure about Hugh's, but they sure looked friendly. And interested.

"Sweetie!" Hugh jumped up from his chair to greet the woman who must have been his daughter. She was freaking gorgeous, with long, swingy, almost-black hair, deep blue eyes, and the lush lips of a young woman. The resemblance to her father was easy to see.

"Saffi, this is Varden Gallagher. Varden, my daughter." Hugh beamed as she extended her hand.

I found myself smiling, too. I hadn't seen anything this sweet and young in far too long, and as she settled in, I noted her rocking body. Maybe it was the whole package —her bright smile, tight jeans, and low-cut halter, but she was cute as hell.

Her father took notice of her outfit, too. "Are you going somewhere after dinner? Because I know you didn't go to work like that."

She smiled, dimples jumping into action. Damn, she was cute.

"You are correct, Dad. I did not dress like this for work." She laughed and shook her head.

"So where are you off to?" Hugh asked.

"Oh, meeting friends," she said a little too quickly.

Meeting friends, my ass.

Her answer might have fooled her dad, but I saw right through it. She probably had a booty call somewhere with some young bastard who wouldn't realize how lucky he was. But the jerk would wake up in a few years and find he was too old to get hotties any longer. Unless he was loaded. With the right amount of money, a guy could have anything.

While Hugh and Saffi bantered, my attention drifted back to the ladies at the bar, who had not stopped staring, not even when Saffi joined us. They couldn't know she was Hugh's daughter, nor did they seem to give a damn.

"Varden, I understand you're one of my dad's clients," Saffi said.

"Varden? Varden, you with us?" Hugh asked.

"What? Oh sorry, so sorry. I was distracted for a moment. Yes, Saffi, my hedge fund firm has been working with your dad since the day we opened. I'd say we make a pretty awesome team." I lifted my glass.

"Cheers to that," Hugh added. We clinked glasses and sucked down the last of our bourbon.

Over our meals, Saffi chattered about her job, which seemed like a good gig even thought the poor kid couldn't afford her own place. That would seriously suck. But Hugh was a cool guy and probably wouldn't have an issue with his daughter running around town like you're supposed to do when you're in your twenties. I smiled, thinking back to those days. I'd gotten a lot of pussy then, but being in my mid-thirties really hadn't slowed me much. Except for that problem of late. I could get it up. Just not off.

Saffi lamented the lousy assignments the paper was giving her as well as other offenses they'd committed against her.

"You know, sometimes people assume you can't be smart when you're as pretty as you are," I offered.

Oops.

If looks could kill. The scowl she sent me reverberated through the restaurant.

Christ. Shoulda kept my mouth shut.

"Yeah, Varden, thank you. That's super helpful," she snapped.

"Saffi, I'm sure Varden did not mean to insult you," Hugh said. "As much as we'd like to believe otherwise, people come with all kinds of preconceived notions and prejudices."

She put her hand on her dad's arm. "I know. Let's change the subject." She threw me serious stink eye.

I'll be damned.

She was a smart kid and knew better than to get into it with one of her father's clients. After all, we were the folks who paid for her college tuition and her dad's trips to the south of France every summer.

Saffi gathered her wrap and purse. "Dad, I hate to eat and run. But I gotta get going. Thank you for dinner." She bent to kiss his cheek. "Nice meeting you, Varden," she said with an extended hand.

Her grip was firm but warm.

Hugh stood to give her a kiss on the cheek. "Be careful out there, baby. It's a wild city."

"I know, Dad. I'm always careful. Love you."

I discreetly watched her small, round ass bounce out of the restaurant. It'd be nice to get to know her better, but that might not be the smartest idea. Even though my twitching cock said otherwise.

"What a great girl. You must be really happy with her," I told Hugh.

"Definitely. Her mom passed when she was only a kid. It's been just the two of us since then. I'd say she turned out all right." His smile said it all.

"Hugh, you see those two ladies at the bar? I think they wouldn't mind having a drink or two with us. Whaddya think?"

Hugh glanced over his shoulder. "Oh, I don't know. I have to do some work for a client meeting first thing tomorrow. Can I get a rain check?" He stood.

I stood, too, grasping his hand. "Absolutely. We'll do it soon."

With Hugh gone, I headed to the bar to make some new friends.

"Ladies. What can I get you to drink?"

My phone rang on the drive home.

"Hello?"

"Is this Mr. Varden Gallagher?"

"Yes, it is. Who's this?"

"The San Francisco Police Department. Your brother, Beaumont, asked us to call you."

Shit. What was he up to now?

"Mr. Gallagher, your brother's been arrested for drunk and disorderly conduct."

"Is he all right?"

"He was in a fight but is okay. Do you want to come bail him out?"

"Yes. Yes, I will. I'll head over right now. Thank you."

I whipped the car around to head for the county jail on Seventh Street. The sad thing was, I'd been there so many times, I actually knew where to find the best street parking.

I headed straight for the *information* window. It was where they always had you start.

"I'm here for my brother, Beau Gallagher."

The clerk couldn't have looked more bored she as she clicked on her keyboard. She handed me some papers and directed me to another window to post bail.

After waiting twenty minutes for my number to be called, I approached the payment window.

"You're bailing your brother out? What a nice man you are," she said.

"Yeah. I guess."

The truth was, I'd been bailing my brother out for a long time, whether it was saving his ass in fights when we were kids, sending him to rehab, or getting him out of jail. The two of us had come a long way from our humble beginnings, but Beau always hovered inches away from slipping into the same alcoholic despair that had ruined our dad's life. And nearly ruined ours.

They escorted Beau to the waiting area. The shame on his face was so painful I looked down at my own feet to give him some relief.

"Var. Thanks," he said in a quiet voice.

I put a hand on his shoulder. "It's all good, Beau. Ready to roll?"

"Yeah. Let's get the hell out of this shithole."

The drive to my place was silent. I didn't need to ask Beau if he wanted to crash at my place for the night—it was what we did when he'd fucked up. He'd come home with me for a day or two and then go back to his own place, clean up, and commit to staying sober until it all went down again.

"Beau, do you mind if I go out for a while?" I asked after he was settled into the guest room.

"Nah, go for it. I'll watch some TV and crash after I clean up."

"I'll see you in the morning then?"

"Sure. And Var?"

"Yeah?"

Beau avoided my gaze, busying himself with the bed sheets. "Um. Thanks."

I nodded. After I'd pulled the apartment door shut, I took a deep breath and headed out for the evening's second act. Time to let off some steam.

CHAPTER 8

SAFFI

I had to admit, I was scared shitless about my next destination of the evening after dinner with Dad, not to mention, a little titillated by Dad's hot friend. What was the guy's name? Oh, right. Varden. He was gorgeous, no doubt, with thick, messy hair, a perfectly chiseled face, and dark, dark eyes. And he'd worn some of the most beautiful clothing I'd ever seen on a man. Certainly nicer than anything I ever saw on the guys I worked with at the paper.

But I knew Varden's type. Hot, rich, man-whore. And commenting on my appearance? What the hell?

It didn't matter. I'd never see him again.

Unless Dad invited him to the firm holiday party...

I got in my car and leaned back on the headrest, eyes closed. With a deep breath, I turned on the ignition.

Let's get this party started.

The instructions for accessing the club had come in a

text message toward the end of dinner. My phone had buzzed, and for a second I was afraid Varden had spotted it. I casually glanced at the message while they discussed some sort of new industry regulations.

I was to arrive at Club Silk and ask for Miss M. The message said the building's street address would not be visible, and to give myself extra time to identify it by looking at the addresses to the right and left. There would be no asking for identification since the club was all about protecting its members' privacy, but I'd have to verbally agree to follow a few, simple rules.

I was to text back with the first initial of my last name.

Sounded easy enough.

I arrived with time to spare and parked a half block away so I could watch other guests come and go. The club was in the old Dog Patch district of the city, which mostly consisted of run-down warehouses and factories, tech startups, and the occasional house inhabited by hipster squatters.

I checked my makeup again and took some deep breaths to calm my nerves. I would *not* let this opportunity slip through my fingers. How many other chances like this would I get at the paper?

What's the worst that could happen, anyway? They'd figure out who I was and kick me out? That would suck, but it wouldn't be the end of the world. Who knew, maybe there'd be a story in *that*.

At two minutes past the hour—I didn't want to look desperate—I climbed out of my Honda Civic. I crossed the street to the club, and discreetly read the buildings' street numbers while strolling.

The club's front door was large, black, and nondescript. The only indication that there was life on the other side was a peephole, and a small, illuminated doorbell. I fluffed my hair, rubbed my teeth clean of lipstick, and put on my best *I own this place* smile.

The door whipped open. I could barely see beyond the glamorous woman facing me.

"You must be Miss M?"

C'mon, confidence.

"Please, come in," she said, nodding.

It took me a sec to adjust to the dim light, but when I did, I took in a room covered in heavy damask wallpaper with pillar candles scattered about and dark, overstuffed furniture, just as I pictured a bordello. And it was pretty damn sexy. A few men and women sat on the sofas, chatting quietly with cocktails in hand. On a small dance floor in the corner, a couple moved to the music while enjoying a passionate kiss. I'd never seen such a collection of perfectly toned, coiffed, and stylish people. How did they pull it all off?

But what was most striking was M, herself. Curls spilled down the back of her silky, green evening dress. Her eyes were ringed in just the right amount of kohl, and her full lips were red and glossy. Her sky-scraping heels put her around six feet tall, something I could easily gauge, being five foot ten myself.

I dutifully followed this thirties-era screen siren to a couple club chairs in a corner.

"Please sit," she said, gesturing. "I understand you'd like to be called B here at the club."

I forced a graceful smile. "Yes, that would be fine." I crossed my legs with my hands around my top knee.

"Very well. And you said you were referred by a friend?" Her head tilted while she smiled coolly.

"Yes, that is correct."

"And who was that friend?"

Oh shit. Of course she was going to ask that.

Think fast.

"I'm afraid I can't share that with you. Sorry."

She looked down at her hands. "All right, B. I would like to stress that Club Silk is an oasis for its members. People come here for many reasons. But one thing they all have in common is a desire to have their privacy protected. Just like you hope for, I assume?"

"Yes, I expect my privacy to be protected." I nodded.

"Then you will verbally agree to never speak of the club when you are beyond its walls. If you see someone outside whom you know from the club, you will not acknowledge them. You will not ask anyone's real name, nor share yours. You'll see that many of the members wear masks. You will respect their desire to keep their faces hidden. All sexual activity—from light touching to full-on intercourse—is completely consensual. You can count on never being pressured by anyone to do anything." She smiled and sat back in her seat.

"Of course, there may be interested parties who will endeavor to seduce you. We all know and enjoy the thrill of the chase," she added.

Damn right.

"May I ask you some questions now?" I ventured.

"You may," she said with a slow nod.

"Is this your place? How long have you had it?"

"B. You will learn all that and more over a period of time as you get to know the club and its members."

She stood. Should I stand, too?

"Now, I'll leave you to explore on your own. If you need anything, please let me know."

She floated away to greet someone else who'd just arrived, her green dress swirling around her lower legs. The new guest was in profile, but wore a full-face mask.

Geez, what was he hiding from?

But more importantly, where could a cool mask like that be found?

I spotted a staircase in the far corner and headed over to it, not wanting to look like a loser sitting all by my lonesome. I needed to get the lay of the land and collect as much detail as I could, as quickly as I could.

Crossing the room, I noticed both male and female heads turning, checking me out. Probably because I was a new face? Or rather, a new piece of ass?

At the top of the stairs, where there was even less light than the first floor, I was offered a glass of champagne, which I reminded myself to drink slowly. I needed to keep my wits about me. A woman wearing a red dress and high heels sat on a cushy sofa. I made a beeline for her.

Maybe she'd be friendly.

"May I sit here?"

"Of course." She patted the seat next to her as she looked up at me. "You're new here."

She was stunning. Black bobbed hair, green eyes, her full lips smeared with nothing more than a neutral gloss.

"Yup. It's my first time."

The woman extended her hand. "I'm P." She held up her champagne glass for a toast.

"I'm B. I'm never gonna keep these one-letter names straight."

P laughed. "Don't worry. No one does." She took a long draw on the last of her champagne and looked around for the server.

"What brought you here?" P asked.

"Oh, I was just curious I guess," I said.

"So you came by yourself? For your first time?" Her eyebrows rose.

Hmmm. Was that why people were staring?

"Sure," I told her. "Why? Is that strange?"

She pursed her lips thoughtfully, and smiled. "I guess it's not strange. It's just that most women are brought here for the first time by a man." She waved over the server for two fresh glasses of champagne.

"Cheers. You've got some balls," P said, holding her glass up.

I laughed, hoping my mirth didn't sound as fake as it felt. But the champagne was helping take the edge off.

"Thank you. Thank you very much."

I spotted another dance floor in the distance, a couple smaller rooms I couldn't quite see into, and a bunch of seating areas like the one P and I were occupying. Beyond that, there was another staircase leading to a higher level.

"Where's that go?" I pointed.

"There are a couple play rooms on the third floor for the super high rollers. Very exclusive. I've been in them a couple times."

"Why do they need their own rooms?"

P tilted her head and made an *I can't believe you asked that question* face. "Wow. You are really green aren't you?"

"So what if I am?"

P sighed. "Some have their own rooms because they have some pretty intense kinks. And some just want an extra layer of privacy. A couple years ago, a guy sneaked some photos with his iPhone and then threatened certain members with blackmail. People fucking freaked out. They stopped coming for a while. I thought the club was gonna close."

"Whoa. What came of it?" My shaking hands sent a splash of champagne onto the sofa. Dammit.

"People gradually came back after Miss M stepped up security. And the guy? Rumor has it he disappeared."

"What? What do you mean, disappeared?"

Jesus, what have I gotten myself in to?

"Well, he never showed his face at the club again. But a couple folks knew him from around town. They said they never saw him again out and about either. His phone was disconnected, his apartment abandoned."

My eyes grew wide with horror. What the fuck?

P smiled, shrugging. "But like I said, that's just a rumor. Probably not even true."

Holy shit.

CHAPTER 9

VARDEN

I t was a relief to get out of the house after bailing out
Beau.

The poor bastard had had nothing but a dark cloud
hanging over his head since he was a kid. It was one of the
reasons I didn't get upset with him when things did
implode for him. Maybe I was an enabler, but I really
believed he was doing the best he could.

Given the circumstances.

Like always, club ritual of pulling my mask on transformed me into a different person—one without a care in
the world. I said my customary hellos on the first floor
and spent my usual five minutes flirting with Miss M,
then wandered up to the mezzanine.

It was early yet.

I inhaled the wood scent of my mask, further chasing
away concerns of the day and erasing, at least for a time,
both the past and future. Wearing it, I existed only in the

moment. And I desperately needed it on a night like tonight, when the past threatened to catch up and take me down.

No one could see my face, no one knew who I was, and no one knew anything about me. I was nobody but G, and that was just how I planned to keep it.

In the dimly lighting, two women perched on the sofa where X, Y, and Z had been the evening before. I passed them on my way to get a bourbon, and threw a small smile in their direction.

I wasn't ready to engage. Hell, I might not be for the entire evening. I was usually all too happy for any hot chick to wrap her lip around my hard dick, but tonight I was feeling mellow. Watching might be the extent of things. Time would tell.

Drink in hand, I settled into a large, comfy club chair in a corner where I figured I'd be left alone, and where I'd have enough privacy to lift my mask long enough for a nice long draw on my liquor.

I tried to get a better look at the two women I'd just passed, but it was hard in the low light. From what I could see, the first, a stunner with short black hair, was a club regular. I'd played with her once or twice. What the hell was her name? With these silly one-letter labels, I could barely keep anyone straight.

I couldn't get a read on the woman opposite her, facing away from me. She had nicely toned shoulders and arms—that much I could make out, thanks to her skimpy top. Thick dark hair spilled in waves down her back. Perfect for grabbing. She ran her hand through it over and over, as if she were nervous.

That sort of vulnerability killed me, and usually ended up working in my favor.

I finished my drink and headed for the third floor. There was probably something going on up there; there always was. I could usually count on seeing some gorgeous thing get pounded by a guy with a baseball bat for a dick. Those scenes often turned into group play.

Great way to get your balls licked, if you were in the mood.

But approaching the stairs, a surprise nearly blasted me off my feet. The women I'd just been checking out were heading upstairs, themselves.

And the one in the halter-top whose face I'd not been able to see?

I knew her. In fact, I'd just seen her one hour earlier.

Holy shit.

She was my *fucking* attorney's daughter. The pretty young thing who worked for the paper. Whom I'd just had dinner with at City Grille.

What was her name again? Susie? Sally? Cindy?

What the *hell* was she doing there? And what would her old man say?

I had half a mind to leave the club. Just go home. Call it a night.

They climbed the stairs, noticing me standing in place, frozen. Thank god for the mask.

"Hi, G," the one with the red lips said.

"Nice to see you," I managed to return.

Hugh's daughter smiled and said nothing.

Saffi. Her name was Saffi.

Dinner ran through my mind again. I hadn't really

paid her much attention, aside from thinking how gorgeous she was and how it might be nice to fuck her, had she not been my attorney's daughter.

Apparently, she was also a kinky little slut.

After my initial surprise and the urge to bolt wore off, I followed them because, of course, who the hell wouldn't? Had she been there before? Was this her first time? And how the hell did she even get in?

I sure liked what I saw, just as I had at dinner. Nice, curvy ass encased in tight jeans, and that low-cut halter showing just enough side boob to reveal some very nice and very real tits.

I pretended I was looking for someone in order to put some distance between us. It wouldn't pay to seem stalkerish. And wouldn't you know it, they headed right for the ultra-private Twist Room.

My Twist Room.

Christ.

They knocked, and the huge bouncer admitted them. He noticed me, too, and beckoned me inside. Men went through all sorts of membership hell to join Club Silk, and even more to have access to Twist. But beautiful women had only to look in the direction of the door, and the discriminating and loyal bouncer not only welcomed them, but also made them comfortable if there was any hesitation—like there was a party inside they couldn't possibly miss.

The door clicked behind us. Time to make my move. Who cared if she was my attorney's daughter? If she had the balls to show up in a place like Silk, she was fair game.

"Ladies. I hope you're enjoying your evening," I said.

"It's been awhile," the one with the lipstick replied.

That's right. She remembers how nicely I fucked her.

"Hello, beautiful," I said to her. "And who is your friend here?"

"Ah. This is...I'm sorry, what did you say your name was?" she asked Saffi.

"I'm B." She extended a hand.

My cock was getting harder by the moment.

"Welcome to the club, B. Is this your first time?"

"Yes. Yes, it is."

Interesting.

"How'd you find out about our little slice of heaven?" I asked.

Nervousness washed over her face. "Oh, um, a friend told me. Word of mouth, you could say."

She was lying. I'd been around long enough to smell bullshit.

"Well, if you have a few minutes, I'd like to get you a drink." Without waiting for an answer, I turned to Red Lipstick. "You wouldn't mind excusing us for a bit, would you?"

Lipstick smiled brightly at me. She was a beauty, no doubt. But she knew the way things worked at the club, and she'd be the last one to cock block me. "Of course, darling." She turned to Saffi. "I'll be right over here, catching up with friends."

She pointed to a tufted mattress where a woman was being fucked from behind by one guy, and in the mouth by another.

Taking Saffi by the elbow, I led her to a small love seat. "Tell me, B, what can I get you to drink?"

She leaned back into the soft cushions, draping an arm over the back. Was she gaining some confidence? Or maybe she was just a mediocre actress.

"A glass of champagne would be great, thank you."

When I returned with our drinks, I sat at the other end of the love seat and turned to face her.

"So, a friend told you about this place. That's interesting," I said.

Her brow furrowed the tiniest bit. "It is? Why?"

"Well, we don't get many new people that way. But it's all good. Don't worry. I'm sure Miss M is very glad to have you."

"Yeah, she sat me down and told me the rules."

"Oh, yes. The goddamn rules. I guess we need a few of those to make a place like this work."

Holy shit. Was I really hanging out with my legal counsel's daughter? In a sex club? If Hugh Bartlett ever got wind of this…well, shit. He was one of the top lawyers in San Francisco.

I could only imagine what he could do if he were pissed enough.

CHAPTER 10

SAFFI

Only fifteen minutes in, but so far, sex clubs rocked. The place was overwhelming. Refraining from staring was simply not possible. I couldn't help myself. In the few minutes I'd been in the Twist Room, the place had filled up. My new friend P's dress was already down around her waist, and a man and a woman enjoyed each of her bare breasts.

Gradually, the dress came completely off, revealing a clean-shaven pussy, which she began to finger with fury.

Jesus. She's gonna come.

I'd never seen a woman orgasm. Well, except in porn, and everyone knew that shit was fake. On top of that, I'd never been with a woman—something I was beginning to think I might be interested in changing.

At the other end of the room, a man lay on his back with a woman straddling his hips. She leaned forward, kissing him. Just behind her was another guy. Holy shit, no way. The guy in back had loaded up his hand and then his cock with a bunch of lube. And now that cock was disappearing into that woman's—ass. Yes, ass.

What a night to remember. For the sake of the paper, of course.

The woman, nearing delirium, moaned loudly. The guys were pretty damn loud, too, with their grunts and groans. I looked around to see if I was the only looky-loo staring, but the three had attracted attention from many in the room.

"You seem to like what you're seeing," my new friend whispered.

No shit.

G—the club nickname of a guy wearing a wild-looking Venetian mask—seemed to have taken a liking to me, at least enough to spirit me away from P.

I turned my attention back to him. "Well, don't you think it's hot? I mean, come on." I gestured to all the people gathered around to watch.

His head twitched the tiniest amount. God, I wish I could have seen his face. I was at such a disadvantage.

He didn't miss a beat. "The first time you see other people fucking, it's kind of shocking. But once you get used to it, it's pretty damn alluring," he said, quietly.

His voice sounded tinny from inside the mask. I guess I understood the desire to disguise one's identity. Indeed, it seemed about half the club felt that way. But it would have been nice to see the man I was speaking with.

"It is pretty amazing," I agreed.

He stood, hand extended. "Let's get a better look."

"Really? It's not, I don't know...tacky?" Someone I'd

not known fifteen minutes ago was inviting me to watch sex.

"It's to be expected, watching and being watched," he said, leading me over to the threesome. "Have you ever been watched?"

Kind of a personal question. But given where we were, it seemed par for the course.

"No," I said, trying to stay cool, like I talked about things like this all the time. "In college, my roommate and I sometimes had our boyfriends stay over at the same time. We'd all be going at it, but the lights would be out." I shook me head. "It was nothing like this, that's for sure."

He laughed. "I remember those days. I guess some things never change."

"What about you?" It was so strange to talk to someone whose eyes were the only thing I could see and barely at that, as dark as it was in the room. No expression to read, no emotion to react to.

He paused before answering me. "I've enjoyed my time as a member of the club. Let's just say that."

The woman just next to me, nude but for high heels, leaned into the man behind her. One of his hands worked its way in and out of her pussy lips, slowing to provide her clit extra attention. She writhed against him, one hand gripping his arm for balance, the other stroking her own breasts.

Another member of the audience had freed his cock from the fly of his trousers and was stroking it in a leisurely rhythm. In the outside world you'd call the cops on that. But at Club Silk, it seemed all bets were off.

The other voyeurs were enthralled, some silent and

awestruck, while others chatted quietly as if they were studying a work of art.

The objects of all this attention, the threesome, seemed not to notice. The woman being pummeled in two places had closed her eyes, having reached another plane of being. She ground onto the cock below her while the one behind slowly made its way in and out of her ass.

How the hell would I put this in my story?

The experience stunned me into an erotic daze. The three were entirely in sync, enjoying their own pleasure as equally as their lovers'. I shifted to get comfortable in my binding blue jeans, and when I looked down, found my nipples jutting hard against my silk top.

I wobbled in my high-heeled boots, and just as wooziness overtook me, G caught my arm and lowered me to a close by sofa.

"Hey, careful," he said, pushing errant strands of hair from my face.

The room was still swirling. "Could I get a glass of cool water, please?" I asked, and leaned my head back on the sofa.

When he returned, he ran a small ice cube over the back of my neck. God, that felt good.

"Thank you. I don't know what happened. I guess it was the champagne, the excitement..." I shook my head to clear the cobwebs.

He ran his palm along my cheek. It felt nice, but with the mask between us, it was oddly non-intimate.

"Why do you wear that?" I asked, running a finger along the filigree trim.

He placed my hand back in my lap. Geez.

"I like my privacy."

"Do you take it off?"

"Nope. Not in the club, anyway."

With the heady setting, coupled with the champagne and G's seductive attentions, I'd nearly forgotten my purpose for being there. "Have you been a member long?" I asked, easing back into reporter mode.

His fingers entwined mine. Smart move, this guy. Make the girl relaxed, admired, and then go in for the kill.

"Nobody knows how long the club has been around. As for me, I've been a member…long enough."

A non-answer answer.

"Okay." Seemed that was all I was going to get. At least for now.

He ran his thumb over my lower lip. His hand smelled like expensive soap, and his rolled sleeves showed a nice, strong forearm, and just the edge of a tattoo.

"What's with all the questions?" he asked. "Are you a private detective or something?"

With the damn mask, I couldn't tell if he was serious or pulling my leg.

I leaned toward him and whispered, "Why yes. I am a private detective. I'm here to gather information on—" I looked for someone to gesture toward. "Him. That gentleman over there."

"Why? What did he do?" He leaned in conspiratorially, playing along.

"Rumor has it…" I paused and looked around for dramatic effect. "That he waters his lawn when California's in a drought."

G laughed from behind his mask, shaking his head.

Whew. Close one.

So far, I hadn't gathered much of anything to build a story around. But I'd gotten a ton of material that I could...um...dream about. That sort of thing.

I stood. Time for good-byes. I saw P on the other side of the room, having fun with a new couple—a very expensively dressed man, and a woman who looked like a model. She moved back and forth between kissing the two of them.

Damn.

I caught her eye, and she waved and blew me a kiss. So I blew one back.

When in Rome...

I turned to G, yawning dramatically. "I need to head home. Early morning."

He stood slowly and tilted his head at me. "I'll walk you out."

As we approached the ground floor, he stopped me on the stairs and seized a shank of hair from the back of my head.

Holy shit.

With a tug, he pulled my head back, holding it close enough to his face that I could hear his breath.

I closed my eyes, tumbling into the sensation of a strange man taking control. And as soon as I did, he spun me around to bend me over the stair railing. With my balance thrown off, there was no choice but to lean all my weight on it. He'd seized the upper hand. Not that I minded.

I hadn't come to play, but if I were an ice queen, wouldn't that raise suspicion?

Oh hell, who was I kidding. I was dying for release. Watching all that fucking was not for the faint of heart, and especially not for someone who badly needed to get off. The atmosphere was irresistible.

I wouldn't have made it home without at least one good orgasm in the car.

"Pull down your jeans," he growled, tightening his grip on my hair.

My hands flew to unbutton my pants. I hesitated and glanced around, seeing people in various stages of undress all around.

So I undid my fly—all in the name of research—and pushed my jeans to just below my ass cheeks.

G followed by hooking a finger in the lace of my thong panty. In an instant, my ass was entirely bare, my sex throbbing from the thrill of exposure.

And strangely, there was no embarrassment. On the contrary, it was empowering. And fucking sexy as hell. Exhibitionism was underrated.

His warm hand ran over my ass, and then *thwack!* He'd smacked my right cheek good and hard. And just when the stinging reached its crescendo, his large palm relieved my burning skin with a soft, smooth touch, calming the fire.

Thwack!

This time he'd smacked my left ass cheek. And again, as my flesh screamed in pain, he soothed me. For a moment, I considered protesting out of decorum, having never been spanked before. But the truth was, I wanted him to continue. It was confusing as hell. The more turned on I got, the more confused I became, vacillating between wondering if our play was okay or whether it was degrading, and admitting I loved it.

His lips touched my ear. "You like that, my little friend? You like having your sweet ass smacked till it's bright pink? You should see it. So pretty, all worked up."

I just nodded. I couldn't speak.

As my flesh cooled, his fingers tickled the crack of my ass. I squirmed from the sensation, earning myself another smack. And then another

I squeezed my thighs together in hope of some relief. But I knew there was only one thing that would help.

CHAPTER 11

VARDEN

Damn if my cock wasn't throbbing and ready to rage. I had Saffi over the railing, ass in the air. Even in the dim light, her pale skin burned bright pink with the outline of my merciless hand.

She responded beautifully to my touch, better than I had even hoped. She was a lean girl, but her behind was pretty as an upside-down heart. A beauty. Supremely smooth and round.

Spanking the ass of my attorney's young daughter. How fucked does someone have to be to do that?

And yet. I guess I had my answer.

"I think you like that," I murmured in her ear, undeterred by any call to reason.

And all she could do was mumble in reply.

My fingers ventured further down her ass, between her legs where they met with hot, creamy wetness. She was soaked.

I wiggled one finger between her pussy lips and found her opening. I entered her just until I heard her gasp and whisper a small "Yes." I slipped another finger in, and she wiggled her hips to drive them deeper.

With a third finger in her, I began to pump. Slowly at first and then faster when she bucked back against my hand.

Fuck, yeah. That's a hot little slut.

"Are you gonna come on my hand, beautiful? C'mon, give me something to lick off my fingers."

Those were the magic words. She pushed so hard against my hand we both nearly fell. I still had a grip on her hair, so her movements were limited, but she bucked like a wild animal, coming, her sex pulsing, her moans catching the attention of the entire first floor.

As her orgasm wound down, I slipped my fingers out. I turned her to face me and wrapped my arms around her so she wouldn't fall.

Unbelievable. My attorney's daughter just came on my hand.

After a moment, she picked her head up from my chest, pushing my arms away. "I have to get home."

She pulled her panties and jeans up, and when she was put back together, she started toward the door.

I reached for her arm. "What are you, Cinderella or something?"

"Yeah. Something like that."

"Can I get your number?"

She looked at me for a second, then reached in her purse and scribbled on a scrap of paper. She thrust it at me and whirled around, almost falling down the last couple stairs.

As she approached the door, Miss M tried to engage her. But she headed her off and disappeared before being trapped by conversation. M's usual languorous expression was replaced by something I'd never seen. Was that worry? Or frustration?

She turned to me.

"Do you know that woman? Tonight was her first night here," M said when she'd caught up to me.

No shit.

I shook his head. "Nope, sorry. Never seen her before in my life."

Next morning, I returned to my office after wrapping up a seven a.m. meeting with our investment analysts. The guys—and one gal—had been working hard, and things were looking good for the firm's upcoming quarter.

I closed my door and crossed to the floor-to-ceiling windows to check out the view of the San Francisco Bay, speckled with sailboats that looked like tiny toys, bouncing around in the choppy water.

I pulled out the piece of paper Saffi had thrust at me the night before. She'd run out of the club like a bat out of hell, which was probably for the best. I didn't trust myself around her. She was young, she was beautiful, and she was off-limits. No way could I fuck around with my lawyer's daughter.

But the piece of paper dangling from my fingers tortured me.

"Yo, boss." My office door flew open, and my business partner, Monty, bounded in. He plopped down on the chair opposite my desk and put a foot up.

"Do you have to put your goddamn shoe on my desk?"

He rolled his eyes and moved his foot. "Sorry, princess, for spoiling your kingdom."

I shoved Saffi's scrap of paper back in my pocket and sat down opposite him. We'd been at graduate school together, worked in investment banking, and later opened our own hedge fund.

"What's up, Mont? How's that new analyst doing?"

His eyebrows rose. "You mean that hot as shit babe that just outshone every guy in the room? Dude, my dick was so hard for her during that meeting. I didn't know how I'd get up and walk out when it ended. She's something."

I nodded, looking at Monty through narrowed eyes. "Remember, we've talked about this. No fucking the chicks in the office. Nothing could bring us down as fast as that kind of bullshit drama."

"I hear ya. Not to worry. I'm keeping it tucked in. But that's not to say some of the younger guys in the office won't go for it. Hell, I would if I wasn't the boss."

"Let the younger guys do what they want. If they get caught up a creek without a paddle, that's not our problem."

Monty glanced at his watch. "So, you joining us tonight to play some ball? I got a court reserved at the club."

I sat back and crossed my legs, one foot placed on the opposite knee. The paper crinkled in my pocket, like it was speaking to me. "I don't know—"

"Oh, come on, man. You're gonna puss out *again*?"

"Would you just relax? I have some things to do." The folded corner of Saffi's phone number poked me through my pants.

"What the hell do you have to do that's so important?" Monty asked with a smirk.

Think fast.

"My brother's had some trouble again." Shit. Using Beau as an excuse? Now that was *bad.*

Monty leaned forward, concern crossing his face. "Oh, Jesus. I didn't know. Sorry."

My office door blew open again. Was there any peace in this goddamn place?

It was my admin. She could barge in anytime she wanted.

"Monty, your nine a.m. has arrived. They're in the conference room."

"Be right there."

Monty stood. "All right, man. Well, maybe you can play next week."

"For sure." I nodded like I'd really go. We did this all the time.

As soon as the door closed and I was alone, I pulled out Saffi's number. I ran my fingers over the ink, as if that would send me some kind of message.

Oh, fuck it.

I entered her number into my phone, and started typing out a text message.

CHAPTER 12

SAFFI

I'd stumbled onto something big.

No, not big. *Monumental.*

My story would shake the city. I'd no longer have to accept crummy little assignments—well, not *all* of them, anyway. They'd entrust me with good, high profile work, and with the chance to prove myself over and over. People would ask my opinion. They'd listen to what I had to say.

But as soon as I was handed the usual list of Chinese food to pick up for the office, I realized my dream was still a ways off.

Ugh.

I went to the Chinese place so often they knew me by name. How sucky was that? *Saffi Bartlett* belonged on the byline of a brilliant piece of journalism, not a hand-written receipt from a takeout restaurant.

Trudging back to the office with multiple plastic bags,

I struggled to hold my head up. It wasn't easy to do when one smelled of fried wontons and sweet and sour pork.

"Saff. Yo, thanks for flying. I'm starved." Tom snatched a bag from my hand and emptied its contents onto the break room lunch table. Chopsticks and fortune cookies clattered to the floor.

Jerk.

"Yeah. You're welcome." I sat next to him. I was hungry, too.

"Geez, Saff," he said, diving into his noodles. "Why so glum?" He tried to hook some of his *lo mein* with his chopsticks, but the slippery noodles slithered right out of them and landed on the grimy table.

"I don't know. I guess it's the job."

This was part of my ploy, to tell no one about the story until the last minute, with the exception of Ed. That would guarantee maximum impact at the paper. They'd all be blown away by my investigative skill *and* writing talent.

I pictured for a moment how great it would be for *someone else* to get the damn Chinese food my coworkers seemed unable to live without.

Seriously. How much lo mein can a person eat?

"Oh, Saff."

Why did that douchebag have to keep calling me that? At one time, I'd thought it cute. Now it was annoying as hell.

"You know," he said, leaning toward me as if in confidence. "Some people are meant to do the serious work. And some people are meant to support us."

Oh, hell no.

"Excuse me?" I leaned back toward him, just inches from his nose.

His head snapped back. "Oh, Saff," he said with a weak laugh. "I was just kidding. You know me."

"Yeah," I said with a fury that surprised us both. "You'd better be fucking kidding." I grabbed a container of *moo shu* pork and returned to my desk before I lost control and dumped the slimy goo over his head.

∼

Happy hour lasted till six p.m., and with just a few minutes left I ordered another beer. I was waiting on my perpetually late best friend, Nelle. She normally arrived when I was on my first drink. But I since I was into beer number two and wondering where the hell she was, I pulled out my phone to track her down.

And to my surprise, there was a text from my new Club Silk friend.

G.

I saved it for later.

I had to get back to Club Silk, and soon. There was no way around it, not that I minded; I'd only just started gathering information, although I sure as hell hadn't planned on hooking up with anyone, especially not my first night there. On the other hand, if I just kept showing up without ever playing with anyone, well, that wasn't going to help me fit in at all.

I had to figure out what to do about G, and sooner rather than later. He'd be there when I went back. Plus, he was sexy as hell even if he did wear that damn mask.

A hand fell on my shoulder, startling the crap out of me.

"Geez," Nelle said, out of breath and flustered. "Why're you so jumpy? Relax."

I waved for the bartender.

"Hey there. You made it just in time." I ordered her a beer with seconds left in happy hour.

"I haven't seen you in ages," she said, getting situated on her barstool. "How's things at the paper?"

"I'm liking it better. I mean, I think I'm going to be getting more challenging work."

Nelle's face brightened. "No kidding! Tell me."

I opened my mouth to tell Nelle everything, but I stopped. No doubt she could deal with it but...way too soon. I didn't want to answer a bunch of questions that I probably wouldn't have answers for, anyway.

So I fibbed. "Well, there's nothing in particular to tell yet. It's just a feeling. I think my editor is listening to me more."

Who wouldn't listen to a story about a freaking sex club?

Earlier that day, Ed had called me into his office.

He'd leaned forward in his chair, hands clasped on his desk. "Saffi, what's up with the Club Silk story?"

"Well, I visited for the first time the other night."

Of course I glossed over the sexy details, explaining I'd not yet gathered much of substance.

"It's going to be a good story," I assured him. "Why do you ask?"

"I don't know. I mean, is this something you should be doing?" He looked around the room as if there were others present, and then said in a conspiratorial whisper. "Should *you*"—he gestured at me—"be going to a *sex club*?"

"Not sure what you're getting at, Ed."

"Maybe next time you go, you should take me with you."

What the fucking fuck.

I forced a small smile in the hope of wiping the tension off my face.

"I've got it under control."

Did he really think she wanted to go to a sex club with him? Jesus.

"Well, all right," he said. "But before all is said and done, someone else will have to go for fact-checking purposes."

"I understand."

Then he pushed back from his desk and stood like he always did when he was ready to end a meeting.

"Okay then. Keep me posted. Good work."

Nelle was shaking my arm. "Hey. Saffi. You with me? You spaced out again."

I realized I'd shredded my cocktail napkin. "Yeah, yeah. Sorry. I have to stop letting work get me down."

Quick save.

"Yeah, you do. Now what about your office crush? What was his name again? Tim?"

"Tom. It was Tom. But he turned out to be a douche."

"Oh, that's too bad. Onward." She raised her beer glass. "Your mom would be proud of your commitment."

A thud landed in my stomach. *Would* she be proud of her daughter investigating a sex club?

"Yeah, I hope so." I stared at the sweat ring my beer left on the bar.

Nelle nodded. "Of course she would be. She'd be proud of the life you and your dad have built. Speaking of which...how is your handsome father?" Her eyes widened.

"My dad is great. You know him. He doesn't mind my crashing at the house. In fact, I think he likes it. And it's nice to have some time with him after being away at school. Not that I could afford to move out, anyway..."

"Hey, don't despair," She said. "You'll be making more money in no time. We'll get a place together."

"Easy for you to say, miss finance major. You've got a great job in banking. But the journalism route does not pay quite as well."

There could be some pretty sweet perks, though. The kind only an exclusive club offered. And I was determined to enjoy them.

CHAPTER 13

VARDEN

I was still busting my ass at the office at seven thirty p.m. when a text finally arrived from Saffi.

Jesus, what was I doing, playing with fire like this?

It was early yet for Club Silk, but I steered my Audi in its direction, anyway. I could get there early, have a drink or two with Miss M, and leave my world behind. No one would need anything from me—not work, not my brother —no one.

With Beau crashing at my place, memories of the tough years with our alcoholic asshole of a father were close at hand. Most days, those fucked-up memories, were far from my consciousness.

But I'd manage to achieve enough, both personally and professionally, to have gotten some perspective on that time. Now if only I could have that same influence on Beau, who'd taken the brunt of the family shitshow.

As the first in the family to make it to college, I was

out of the house when things had gotten their worst. Beau had had to face it all on his own. For that, I'd never forgive myself. He'd been paying for it ever since.

The gift that kept on giving.

I parked a half block from the club. Close, but also far enough to assess the neighborhood, which could be dicey. And most importantly, to watch the comings and goings.

While I cooled my heels, I scrolled through my text messages. Saffi's had been noncommittal as hell. Leave it to a newspaper reporter to not give anything away.

Who knew whether she'd be there later? It would be nice, sure. She was a total hottie with that long, dark hair and pretty, round ass. And the way she'd responded to me. I got hard just thinking about it. But in her absence, I'd probably just hit on someone else. I could be an asshole that way.

Why the fuck was I even thinking about her? Maybe I saw something of myself in her, how she was determined to make her own way?

Whatever.

I rang the club's bell as soon as my mask was on.

Miss M stood before me in another of her slinky gowns—this time blue—her signature long hair in waves and bright red lips. Being greeted at the door was a nice perk, even if she was a little over the top with drama.

"G! So good to see you," she purred, kissing the lips of my mask. She hooked her arm in mine, and we headed for the bar.

"What can I get you, my friend?" she asked, head tilted.

"Thanks. I'll have my usual. A bourbon. On the rocks."

She waved over the bartender, who was still setting up for the evening. "Two bourbons, please."

She leaned back against the bar, propping her elbows on the surface behind her. "I've got something I want to talk to you about."

Hmmm. "What's that, M?"

"That woman you were with the other night. I think her name was B? I want to find out more about her."

Now that was a funny coincidence. Or was it?

"Will you help me?" she asked.

"I don't know. I mean, you know me, M. I keep my privacy protected." I gestured to my mask. "And I don't intend to impose on anyone else's. That's not how I roll."

Good save.

Annoyance crossed her face. She wasn't used to being told *no*. But she quickly reverted back to her sweet smile.

"Of course, G. I completely respect that." She moved closer, lowering her voice even though no one was in earshot.

"But I want you to know, I don't have a good feeling about her. You do what you want, but I'm asking you to be careful."

Thank goodness she couldn't see the expression on my face. She was freaking paranoid. Or, was it good instinct, honed by years of protecting the club?

But Safe was a reporter after all. Could M smell it on her?

I'm sure that had nothing to do with Saffi's attendance at the club. She was hardly Woodward and Bernstein. She wrote about Little League, for god's sake.

"Gotcha, babe." I clinked her glass and headed for the stairs before she killed my buzz.

I parked myself on the cushy second floor sofa where I hoped for a little time to myself, or to be approached by some horny, good-looking chick.

I was flexible.

Turned out, I didn't have to wait long. A tall redhead wearing only stilettos, a thong, and a half mask paraded by, throwing me a little smile. Her ass jiggled just the smallest amount as she walked away, and my cock jerked to life in my trousers.

CHAPTER 14

SAFFI

I killed some time gabbing with Nelle until it was a reasonable hour to make an appearance at Club Silk. I yawned to kick off my exit. "Gosh, I'm pooped."

"Me, too. Let's take off," She agreed.

We headed for the door, but before reaching it, I stopped.

"You know what, Nelle? Before I hit the road I'm gonna visit the ladies' room." I gave her a quick peck on the cheek, and we went our separate ways.

In the restroom, I dug into my makeup bag and proceeded to remove my working girl face and replace it with…what? My sex club face? I carefully re-did my makeup with an eye to creating a sexy, dramatic look. The YouTube videos I'd watched on applying "evening makeup" were paying off. I didn't look like a harlot, at least I didn't think so, but I didn't look like a nun, either.

I pulled a small can of hairspray out of my purse and

shot it over the top of my hair. As it dried, I brushed and teased it into something I hoped was alluring. It was the best I could do.

Done primping, I headed out. The bartender did a double take at my quick makeover.

Whatever, dude.

On the drive across town to the old warehouse district, I couldn't decide whether I was scared, nervous, or excited. Now that I'd been to the club once, I knew better what to expect, and in some ways that was *more* intimidating.

Regardless, I had a good feeling, despite a crappy day at work. Things could be worse. I could be heading to a baseball game for eight-year-olds. Instead, I was going to a freaking *sex club*. Wait until the rest of the paper found out how ballsy I was, and how well I could write a story.

At a costume store, I'd found one of those cool Venetian half-masks some of the others at the club wore. It was painted with a crackly effect intended to make it look old and was embellished with gold swirls, crystals, and glitter. At the center top, a fleur-de-lis ornament soared several inches above my head. It was super cool and made me exotic and mysterious.

I rang the bell, and just like last time, was admitted by Miss M.

"Why, B! Lovely to have you back. Oh, and look at your mask. So glamorous," she said.

"Thank you. I'm excited about trying it out."

I adjusted the mask until it was comfortable and I could see as well as could be expected. Clearly, I'd need to be careful on the stairs. And other places. I didn't want to step on any body parts.

"I understand a sense of anonymity can be very free-ing," I said.

Okay, I pulled that one out of my ass.

"I could not agree more," M said, stepping closer.

She bordered on creepy, no question about it.

"I was hoping that sometime this evening you might accompany me to my office for a little chat. We can get to know each other better."

What? Why?

"That would be great, Miss M," I said with a cool smile, hoping I was successfully hiding my unease.

I placed a hand on her arm, like we were total buds. "Now, if you'll excuse me, I'm in the mood to...explore."

Oh yeah.

After that mini convo with Miss M, my confidence was wobbly. But I guessed I figured if I could handle her, the rest of the scene would be a piece of cake. So I strolled through the place like I owned it, carrying a confidence I was missing in my first visit. For one, I knew what to expect, and two, being incognito rocked. The ability to wear a mask—and a glamorous one at that—brought new meaning to my undercover investigation.

The first floor, in all its velvet glory, was getting a bit crowded for my tastes, so I wove through the bodies to get to the mezzanine.

The open stairs provided a perfect view of the club-goers below, so I stopped to take it all in.

In one quiet corner, a woman in nothing more than high heels rode a man seated on a giant, plushy chair. He was completely dressed except for the trousers puddling around his ankles. His gaze was locked with hers in a combination of wonder and satisfaction. I slowed my ascent as the man's expression morphed, his teeth gritted, lips bared, hollering, "Oh, fuck, yeah."

I'd been holding my breath watching them, and when I finally took a deep inhale, I unclenched the fists that had pressed my nails into my palms. Could I be that woman, having great sex with a guy who adored me?

I finished my climb to the second floor on shaky legs, but not before I saw that others had also stopped to watch the flushed and sweaty pair.

Who could tire of watching a hot couple get it on?

The second floor mezzanine wasn't crowded, at least not yet, and the bartender looked bored out of his mind. His face brightened when I approached him. "What will you have, my lovely lady?"

"Hi. I'll have…some bubbly, if you don't mind."

"Coming right up," he said, reaching into the cooler.

As he went through the motions of serving me, I decided to try my luck at getting some info out of him.

He handed me a champagne flute.

"Thank you." I tried to be flirty and demure. "What's your name?"

"All the help are called O," he said with a smile. "And you are?"

"I'm B."

He extended his hand. "Hello, B. Welcome. You're new, aren't you?"

"I am. How long have you been working here?"

"Couple years."

I nodded as if that were super interesting.

"Cool," I said, nodding. Maybe I could get him to tell me more. "This place is great. How long has it been around?"

"Not sure." He shrugged.

Not sure, my ass.

He grabbed his bar rag and began wiping at some invisible dirt, gradually moving farther away from me, toward the other end of the bar.

So much for that.

CHAPTER 15

VARDEN

"Jesus, you can suck cock," I murmured to the redhead between my knees.

Her gaze met mine, but for obvious reasons, she couldn't speak. She'd beckoned me to follow her to one of the playrooms with a stage in the middle, where she positioned me in a cushy chair.

Who didn't love a woman who took charge?

She'd fished my cock out, rock-hard and aching by the time she got her hands and mouth on it. When she went for the drop of precum on my tip, her tongue was so exquisite it was painful.

I sank into the chair's expensive, down-stuffed cushions and dropped my head back, but not for long—I loved watching. Nothing turned me on more. That's why I liked the club, I suppose. Watch, be watched. It was all good.

The redhead—damn, what was her name, again?— deep-throated me like a goddamn champ. In her bent-over state, her nearly naked ass waved in the air, and a couple men happening by stopped to admire her goods. One shot me a thumbs-up before he moved on. The other seemed to want in on the action, unable to remove his gaze from her pretty ass.

I gestured him over with a wave, and tapped the redhead on the shoulder. She looked up, surprised.

He took the opportunity, as I'd hoped he would, to dive in.

"Baby," he drawled. "I'm dying to lick your tight, little asshole. Would you kindly oblige me?"

Awesome—a preppy, southern perv. There went that whole *telling a book by its cover* thing. Passing this guy in the street, one might think he was on his way to the golf club from his home with his pretty wife and two pretty children.

And maybe he was.

"Yeah," the redhead murmured. "You can fuck me with your tongue." And she got back to eating my cock.

It didn't get much better than that. Watching a gorgeous woman bobbing up and down on my dick while she was about to get her rear pummeled by some guy's tongue, and god knew what else, was pretty special. If I did say so myself.

As the preppy guy arranged himself behind her, the expression on his face was one of pure ecstasy. I'd say that was a true ass man, if ever there was one.

He got to work, and whatever he was doing back there had the redhead squirming out of her skin. This left me the happy beneficiary of her enthusiasm—she sucked me so hard, tears poured from her eyes. My ass-man buddy glanced over at me, and I threw him a little nod. It was the least I could do. He disappeared back behind the cheeks of her ass.

My balls started to tingle and pull in tight, usually a good sign that ecstasy was right around the corner. The red head kept going, bless her.

But it was to no avail.

I couldn't fucking come.

Again.

I reached to ease her off me and realized the preppy dude had taken matters into his own hand. He was busy yanking his hard dick, and just in time, the redhead turned and consumed the guy's load of cum.

We'd amassed a small audience. I pulled myself back together and helped the redhead, who was so woozy she could barely stand. In all the excitement, everyone seemed oblivious to my little problem.

But I wasn't.

Among the crowd stood Miss M and the usual cast of characters. But in the back was a woman in a half mask, standing alone—strange for the club. I couldn't see much more than that in the dim light, but it seemed like she was staring directly at me. There was something about her, but what it was, I couldn't be sure.

I got the redhead settled and looked back at the woman in the mask. I wanted to meet her.

But she was gone.

CHAPTER 16

SAFFI

I could have sworn G saw me watching him, and maybe he had, but I had my mask on. He couldn't have known it was me.

I was getting nervous for nothing.

It wasn't that I didn't want to see him—I just didn't want to see him *that* night. I had work to do.

And as I left the playroom, guess who stopped me. Yup. Miss M.

"Hi," I said, looking down at the hand she'd planted on my arm.

Deep breath.

"Are you having a nice evening?" she asked.

"Oh yes, very nice. That was some show in there, wasn't it?"

M's hand remained on my arm. "Would you come to my office for a little chat? I'd like us to know each other better."

Shit.

But I knew better than to resist. Now was not the time to raise suspicion.

"Sure. I'd love to see your office." And maybe learn a thing or two...

She led me through the club, stopping to say hello to what seemed like a hundred people. I had to hand it to her, though, she introduced me to all of them, which could really come in handy at some point.

The office looked exactly as one might expect. A huge, heavy desk dominated the room, which was decorated with flocked wallpaper, thick red carpeting, a Victorian-style love seat, and a matching chaise. The walls were packed with bookcases, but it was too dark to see any of the titles. *Sex club chic* I guess you would call it.

The stories these walls could tell...

I relaxed on a settee and she walked over to a liquor cabinet.

"Can I pour you some port?"

I hated port.

But without waiting for an answer, she selected an ornate decanter and began pouring the thick red liquid into tiny stemmed glasses.

I accepted it, all smiles, and took a sip, holding my breath.

"So tell me," she said, "what brings you to Club Silk?" She took a seat on the other end of the settee.

I set down my glass. "Well, I suppose I come here for the same reason everyone does."

One of her eyebrows shot up. "Really? I thought people came here for a variety of reasons."

I shot right back at her, "What brings you here night after night? I mean, we know you're the proprietor, but what do you like about it?"

She gave me a smile that said *I see what you're doing here*, set her glass down, and moved closer to me.

"I just want to make sure you're here for the right reasons." She removed my mask and pushed a strand of hair behind my ear.

She dramatically snapped her hand back. "I'm sorry. I shouldn't have been so forward. Did you mind that?"

I shook my head. I actually didn't mind it.

What I did mind, though, and what was getting under my skin, was how sly she came off. She was up to something.

Course, I was up to something, too.

"Good. Very good," she said.

I breathed her light perfume, and then her lips were on mine, soft and light.

I'd kissed a girl only one other time on a dare at a college party. There'd been much alcohol involved.

If she was testing me, I planned to pass with flying colors.

She pulled back and examined my face. "You see, it's my job to make sure my guests are comfortable, and enjoying themselves," she explained.

"That's good of you, M," I said. "I appreciate your looking out for me, and for making sure I settle in well."

She suddenly stood, extending a hand to pull me to my feet. Guess my little test was over.

Had I passed?

"Let's head back to the party, shall we? I have guests to check on, and you need a cocktail."

I replaced my half mask and followed her, leaving the awful port behind. Music blared a thumping dance beat, bodies writhed on the floor, and people fucked on a high stage overlooking the room.

M disappeared into the crowd.

Good riddance.

It was obvious she was trying to scare the shit out of me, intimidate me—the question was, why? She couldn't possibly know I worked for the paper. And the funny thing was, *that* was what scared me.

Or was she just pulling some alpha-girl bullshit?

I worked my way through the crowd toward the bar and ordered my usual bubbly. Rooting through my purse for a cash tip, I saw my phone flashing with a notification a text had just come in.

CHAPTER 17

VARDEN

As soon as the redhead had recovered from having her mouth and ass delighted, I excused myself. Luckily, the preppy perv had grabbed our friend's attention and was now chatting her up, enabling my easy escape.

I wandered through the club, finally cooling behind the mask, and pissed as hell I hadn't been able to come. This was one of those times I really wanted to take the damn thing off. The consequences, though, would be so serious that I never actually did. I'd worked my ass off to build my company, and my weakness for kink was not going to ruin it.

I ordered a drink while I was cooling off, and glanced down from the mezzanine. Miss M and some others who'd been watching me navigated the last step. She was with—wait a minute—she was with the woman with the half mask who'd seen watching me from the back of the room. But before I could make a move, they'd exited the stairs and turned the corner. I tried to follow, but when I reached the bottom of the stairs, I'd lost them.

Damn.

So, I went back up, all the way to the third floor, to the Twist Room. I knocked on the door and the usual over-sized bouncer let me in.

"How are ya?" I extended my hand.

"Mr. G, my friend. So good to see you," he answered with his gap-toothed smile.

"There're some hotties in here tonight, G. Git it."

"Seriously," I said, patting him on the shoulder.

I honestly wasn't up for any more playing, the redhead having sucked the energy out of me—minus the orgasm—but I was always game for watching. I settled into a club chair so no one could sit next to me, and watched the scene taking place just to my right.

Some lucky bastard had two gorgeous women. The blonde with her hair piled on her head—what did they call those? Buns?—was full-figured with flawless skin. The other had a dark-brown pixie cut and was boyishly thin with tits topped in tight, pink nipples. The contrast between the two was extreme, and yet they moved on the man in perfect rhythm.

And he looked to be having a pretty damn good time, too, laying on his back with the skinny one riding his tongue.

At the other end of him, the voluptuous one kneeled, ass in the air, his cock in her mouth, hoovering him like he was her last supper.

The skinny one started bucking on his face,

convulsing with barely a sound as her face twisted. The big-titted one sucked until the guy's legs spasmed. He thrust his hips into her face one last time and began to shoot. She pulled back and let his load coat her full tits.

The hot scene brought Saffi to mind. My new "friend," who also happened to be the daughter of an important business associate. I kept reminding myself of that piece.

But she'd been so responsive when I finger-fucked her, and she was gorgeous to boot. I grabbed for my phone. Maybe she could be persuaded to come out and play?

I texted, and she shot me down, taking a rain check, possibly for tomorrow. It was just as well. I was getting tired and needed to get home to check on my brother, Beau.

CHAPTER 18

SAFFI

I found a private corner to read my text from G.

how r u tonight?

My heart thumped in my chest, and I casually looked around. With the mask, I had to be safe, right? He couldn't identify me. I hoped.

I readjusted my disguise and casually looked through the room. He was nowhere in sight.

was hoping you'd come to the club tonight

Sipping my bubbly, I scoured the room again.

Tomorrow? I asked.

what time?

the usual? I responded.

I dropped the phone back into my purse. The night was young, and I had more investigating to do. The trick was to do it without G identifying me. If he were still there.

I turned to see M with a small group of people, chatting as she watched me from across the room.

Why was she always on my ass?

Smiling, I saluted her and headed for the stairs. Time to see what was going on in the playrooms.

It was my second night at the club, and I barely knew any more than the day the tattered business card landed under my shoe at the bus stop. Well, except that I liked being finger fucked in public, enjoyed kissing another woman, and still hated port.

The club's secrets were sealed up tight. Just like Miss M wanted it.

I needed to find a "friend" to hang with, someone other than G, who might answer some questions. I found a spot on a cushy love seat on the third floor, and figured that soon enough someone would join me.

"Hey," said the bartender from earlier.

"Hi there, O."

He plopped down next to me.

"You're done working?" I asked.

He smiled, displaying some of the deepest, hottest dimples I'd ever seen. I hadn't paid his looks much attention before, but I had to admit that his chiseled jaw and mussed hair were a treat for the eyes.

"Yeah," he said, nodding. "My buddy's got me covered for the rest of the night."

Perfect. He could be my cover just long enough to help me fit in. And maybe provide some info this time.

"So, earlier, I asked you how long the club had been around. Why did you not want to talk to me?"

He shifted on the sofa, turning to face me. "Huh? Oh, I

don't know anything about the place, really." He ran a finger down one of my bare arms, stopping at the crook of my elbow. My nipples sprang to attention.

I suppressed a shiver. Tickling drove me crazy.

He reached past my mask for a piece of hair and fingered a long curl, twisting it around his finger. "What's your name again, gorgeous?" His eyes washed over me, leaving me weak.

"B. I go by B."

Shit, this guy was hot.

Remain focused. This was *work*.

"I mean, I have a real name. That I use in the real world." Why was I babbling?

"Um, yeah, I figured B was just your club name." He smiled. Goddamn those dimples. "B, I'd like to kiss you. Would that be all right?"

"I suppose so."

"You want to take off your mask first?"

"No. No, I do not. But thank you for asking."

He gave a small laugh and leaned in. He was so close the heat of his lips radiated, even though we'd yet to make contact.

Shit, what was he waiting for?

His velvety lips fell on mine, and they tasted so goddamn good. Sort of like expensive scotch and something minty. Falling into him, I parted my lips to taste his tongue.

It was beginning to seem like journalism was a great profession. I giggled into his kiss.

He drew back slightly. "Did I tickle you?" He looked so sincere.

"A little. It's okay." And my mouth fell on his again to do some exploring of its own. Heat rose through my core, and all thoughts of work fluttered away. I squirmed in my seat, my panties soaking with my pleasure.

"Well," the bartender said abruptly, looking at his watch.

Huh?

He stood. "I'll see you next time, then?"

"Um. Yeah. Sure," I said.

"Super." He smoothed back his hair. "Have a good night." And he was gone.

What a weird freaking place.

CHAPTER 19

VARDEN

I pulled the Audi into my parking garage and locked my mask in the glove box, double and triple checking that it was secure. Yeah, I was that insane about my privacy, I'll admit it.

On the way to the penthouse, I leaned my head back against the elevator wall. Why did I do this to myself, stay out late when I knew I'd be exhausted the next day?

Light glowed from under the guest room door, and the TV played a game show. I knocked lightly.

"Beau? You up?" I called.

A stirring sound came from the other side. "Yeah, c'mon in," he answered in a groggy voice.

He clicked off the TV and propped himself up in bed, running his fingers through his shoulder-length hair. He pulled an elastic off his wrist and gathered it into a short pony tail.

"Guess I fell asleep." He looked everywhere except at me. "I'm sorry about this, you know, everything."

"Yeah. What happened?" I asked.

"I'm not sure. I was out and felt really down, so stopped by a bar. I was gonna have only one..." His voice trailed off.

I sat on the edge of the bed. "You know it doesn't work that way."

He ran a hand over his face. "I know. I fucked up."

"Well. You want some water or juice?" I offered.

"Nah, I'm good."

The shit he'd gone through. Kind of broken my hard as stone heart.

"Hey, I can pay for you to go back to that rehab place you liked. It was much nicer than that halfway house you're in right now," I offered.

"I know. I appreciate it." He nodded, then finally looked at me. "But you can't just keep throwing money at me and my problems. It's not that simple."

This was a familiar conversation.

"I don't throw money at you. I want to help."

"Var, you are a fucking rock star, and I'm your loser little brother. It's just the way it is. You can't spend your way out of this," he said.

"That's bullshit and you know it. We might just as easily have ended up in each other's shoes. You could have been the successful one, and I could have been the one who's a mess. So much of life is a fucking crapshoot."

I looked my brother and saw the scared little guy I'd left behind when I escaped to college. At that moment, I hated myself more than he hated himself, if that were possible.

There was nothing fair about life. Not a goddamn thing.

"I'm not giving up on you. Even if you give up on yourself."

Beau looked at his hands and said nothing.

"G'night, bro." I switched off the light and closed the door. I had to get out of there.

CHAPTER 20

SAFFI

I sat in front of a blank computer screen most of the day, unable to write a damn thing. Ed had inquired about my progress on the Club Silk story, so of course I lied.

Aside from describing the physical setting, there wasn't much to say. I'd gotten pretty much zero information from the folks I'd met. 'Course, I could always share some of my *personal* experiences, but I wasn't writing for *Penthouse, now* was I?

Maybe I should be, though.

"Hey."

My heart slammed against my chest and I shrieked. Christ, it was Tom. What did he want? "You scared the shit out of me."

He wrinkled his nose. "Why the hell are you so jumpy?" He craned his neck to see what was on my computer monitor, but I switched windows.

"I was deep in thought."

He helped himself to a corner of my desk, propping his ass right on the story I'd written about Little League.

"So," he said, "Ed tells me you have something very special in the works."

What. The. Hell.

My gaze wandered around my desk to make sure any revealing papers were out of sight.

"Really? Huh." I smiled and shrugged.

"You don't have anything up your sleeve?" He reached for a strand of my hair, but I smacked his hand away, rolling my chair until I was out of his reach.

"Nope. No idea. Don't know why he'd say that to you." I threw my hands up.

Disappointment ran across his face. "Oh. Okay then. I guess you're just still doing your Little League and Garden Club bullshit."

Dick.

"So it would seem."

He started inching away. "Well. I gotta get back to work." He turned to go.

"Tom?"

"Yeah?"

"Thanks for stopping by." I gave him the fakest sweet smile I'd ever mustered.

"Sure thing." He paused by the entrance to my cube. "Hey. Some of us are going for drinks after work. You're invited."

"Oh. Thanks. I'd love to go. Let me check and see if I can pull it off."

"Okay. Later, then," he said.

I turned back to my PC, motivated by Tom's fake interest and explicit insult. The jerk seemed happy I might still be stuck working on the same old crap I always was assigned.

Truth was, I had no intention of getting drinks with Tom or anyone else in the office. Getting ready for a night out at the club was a lot of work. I had a mani-pedi to take care of, and it took forever to blow out my hair. Fortunately, I'd gone for an excruciating Brazilian wax a couple days ago, my first and probably my last, so I was good in that department.

The phone killed my daydream.

"Hey, girl," I said when I saw it was Nelle.

"You will not believe this…" Her voice was breathy.

"Believe what? Tell me."

"Remember I told you about that guy in my office? Around the same time you told me about the guy in your office you were crushing on?"

"Yeah, but I'm not into that guy any more—"

"Well," she said, "he asked me out!"

"Oh my god, that's awesome. I'm very happy for you, sweetie."

She'd liked that guy for so long I thought they'd be in nursing homes before he took her frequent and obvious hints.

She let out a long, relieved breath. "We're going out next week. I'm so happy. I have to figure out what to wear. Hey, what are you doing? Wanna get a drink after work?"

"Ohhhh. Can't. Sorry."

"Why? You got something going on?"

"Yeah, I gotta do some work." It was only a partial lie. I

was obsessed with my story and couldn't think of anything else.

"All right. Well, that sucks. Call me tomorrow?" she asked.

"Of course. Talk to ya later."

I swiped the phone closed. I had to stay focused. I'd created a big expectation with Ed, and coming up empty-handed would be worse than bad. Especially when he had his own healthy dose of curiosity about Club Silk. I needed to get the story done before he insisted on going there some night. With me.

On my bus ride home after work, the butterflies started. What the hell was I doing? Trying to make a name for myself with a story about a sex club would certainly put my name in the spotlight—but would it be the right kind of spotlight?

I couldn't very well go in there with a notebook and tape recorder. That would not be *undercover*. And if I weren't undercover, they would never let me in, and if I didn't blend in and experience the club like a member, well then how the hell would I report on it?

Okay, a lot of reporting was done by observing. I didn't have to play in the Little League to cover their season. I didn't have to belong to the Garden Club or even *have* a garden to write about those old blue-haired ladies.

I suppose I could go to Club Silk and just sit in the corner and watch. Was that what I *should* be doing?

By the time I reached my stop at the end of the line,

the lurching of the bus and my nerves left sweat pouring down my temples. I'd never been so happy to step into the blustery San Francisco fog. Time to get in the house and get ready for a night out.

"Hey there," my dad hollered when I slammed the front door.

I poked my head into his study. He leaned back in his chair, hands behind his head.

"Hey, Dad."

"How was work today?" he asked.

"Good. You know, just starting to work on my story about that...club."

"Oh yeah. How's that going?"

I hated lying to my dad. "Well, the story is different than what I initially shared with you. It's...a bit more involved."

"Oh? Tell me."

I looked down at my fidgeting hands. "I can't really share much. It's kind of undercover."

"Wow. Exciting. I can't wait to read it."

"Dad," I asked, looking up at him, "do you miss Mom?"

He gave me a small smile and rocked his head back and forth. "Every day. Why do you ask? You okay?"

"Yeah. I'm fine. I just hope she'd be proud of me."

"Are you kidding? I *know* she would. I think she'd be proud of both of us, and how we kept each other moving forward after she passed."

The lump in my throat choked my words. "Thanks. I think so, too."

"Hey, do you want to go out for a bite to eat? You hungry?"

I cleared my throat. "Oh, thank you. You know, I'm going out in a bit. Gonna…meet some friends."

"Okay, then. I might get a burger." He stood and grabbed his jacket. Walking around his massive desk, he gave me a kiss on the head. "If I don't see you later tonight, I'll see you in the morning."

"Thanks, Dad. I love you."

"Love you, too, Saffron."

Only my mom had ever called me by my full name.

Mom, are ya with me on this?

CHAPTER 21

SAFFI

A couple hours later I headed across town in the direction of Club Silk. My nerves were firing at full speed, suggesting that bailing on the evening seemed like it might be a good way to go.

But I couldn't do that.

No. I had to go. If I didn't, I might be stuck as the office gopher for eternity, covering "breaking news" from Little League and the Garden Club. I might get stuck doing those things anyway, at the rate I was going. But at least if I tried, could come away with a new friend. Or two.

G's mask flashed across my thoughts.

A replay of Miss M's kiss of the previous night sent a shiver down my spine. She was mysterious, even scary. But I had to admit, the kiss had been hot as hell.

Then there was G. Why was I eager to see a man whose face I'd never laid eyes on? Sure, he was sexy and knew his way around a woman's body. And yet, he kept wandering in and out of my thoughts.

I left my car in the closest spot I could find to the club's front door. I was already tempting fate enough— why risk trouble in a dicey neighborhood?

As usual, Miss M answered the door in all her dramatic glory.

"B. My beautiful friend." She welcomed me with a broad sweep of her arm. "So good to see you tonight."

"Thanks M," I said as I pulled on my mask. I was beginning to understand why G wore his. It really was like a security blanket. Or a wall, depending how you looked at it.

"You're not going to cover that pretty face of yours, are you?" she asked.

"First of all, only *half* my face is covered. As you'll see, my lips are still available."

Damn, I was getting good at this.

I stepped closer to her. Time to lay it on. "And second, I like being somebody different for a moment in time."

She smiled and ran a hand around my waist. "I know exactly what you mean."

I looked around the first floor at the party already in full swing. People dancing, flirting, making out. My heart pounded in time to the bass-heavy house music and the sexy buzz in the air. An expensive perfume drifted by.

M fluttered off to greet another guest.

I wasn't exactly an old pro at this sex club thing, but at least I pretty much had the lay of the land down. I got myself some bubbly, which gave me time to scope out the happenings. G was supposed to be there, but I doubted he'd recognize me—he hadn't the other night—which gave me time to snoop around untethered. I'd make myself known to him when I was ready to, and in the meantime enjoy the party. And of course, gather information for the story.

I couldn't forget about the story.

Drink in hand, I squeezed between the packed bodies on the first floor. As usual, there wasn't a ton of playing going on; most people seemed to save that for the smaller rooms. Perhaps the intimacy of those spaces, like the one where I'd seen G, lent themselves to really getting down and dirty. In the open space of the first floor, people for the most part mingled, aside from the few couples kissing in dark corners. Hardly anything to waste one's time watching.

Was I becoming jaded or what?

As I climbed the steps to the mezzanine, I had an unspoiled view of the crowd below. M stood chatting, all Hollywood glamour in her cream-colored gown, watching me from the far side of the club. She raised her glass to me. I raised mine back.

Once upstairs, I scanned for G. I wanted to see him before he saw me, and I waved at the bartender who'd run off the night before.

No G, at least not yet.

I roamed past the dance floor and toward a small room I'd never seen. My mouth fell open.

In it, there were eight or so women in various stages of undress—some of them with thigh highs and boots, others with leather bustiers, and still others with lacy boy shorts and sky-high stilettos. They lay on silky tufted mattresses in a tangled pile of limbs—fingers and tongues exploring. I drifted in for a closer look.

There were no men in sight.

Two women were doing sixty-nine. The woman on top buried her tongue in her partner's sex, causing the woman on the bottom to scream and thrash.

Another woman, on her own, slid a clear glass dildo coated in lube up and down her wet slit, her head writhing in delight.

I turned as a woman stepped into something with straps and buckles, tightening both to take up the slack. Holy shit. It was a strap on, and she began to stroke like it was her own cock.

CHAPTER 22

SAFFI

I was so blown away by the hot as hell girl-on-girl scene unfolding before me that I nearly missed the vibrating phone in my skirt pocket.

I tore myself away from watching the woman using a strap-on, glancing back as I left. I had to admire their complete dedication to pretending the big faux-penis was a real, live cock. After all, they'd stroked and sucked it like it was. And then, fucked each crazy other with it.

you coming? a message from G said.

Was he already there? And if so, where? I looked around in panic but his distinctive mask was nowhere in sight.

almost there, I lied. I needed time to run to the ladies' to rinse off the sweat I'd accumulated. And of course hide my mask.

I finger combed my hair and touched up my lipstick. Hid the mask in my purse. Ready to go.

I headed for the first floor, with no idea where G might have been, to try and pretend I was just arriving. And there was M, watching me, like always.

Did she know something?

But I ignored her. From my position on the stairs, I evaluated the floor below. No sign of G. He wasn't likely on the third either since that seemed to be where the hard-core partiers hung out. I ventured back to the second, where I approached the bartender I'd kissed the night before.

I beckoned him closer with a finger. He didn't recognize me without my mask, which was just as well.

"Hey, maybe you can help me find a friend. His name is G, and he wears a full-length mask. Venetian style."

The express on his face changed, becoming downright unfriendly. "Sorry. Can't help you."

Whoa.

I poured on what hoped was just the right amount of indignation.

"Relax. I didn't ask for his name or social security number. I'm supposed to meet him here for a date." I dramatically stormed away from the bar.

What was with the place and its damn secrets?

I wandered around the floor, casually poking my head into one party room after another. Just as I was about to give up and text him to set up a rendezvous point, I spotted him near the same bar I'd just left. He was facing away, which was perfect.

I could watch him.

Naturally, he was wearing his mask. He watched the

people filing by, occasionally nodding at someone or raising his glass in a toast.

But a tap on my shoulder distracted me.

"B, my dear friend," M said in her warm, dripping voice. "Having a good evening?"

What did she want *now*? I took a deep breath to conceal my irritation.

"What can I do for you, M?" I asked impatiently.

Her head snapped back at my tone, which was fine with me. The last thing I wanted was for her to think she was getting to me.

"Why are you watching G? I'm not sure I'm comfortable with your behavior," she said sweetly.

Passive aggressive bitch.

"I'm meeting him tonight, and was thinking about how gorgeous and mysterious he was." I faced her head on. "Is there something wrong with that?"

She ran her hand up my arm, and up to my face, where she cupped my cheek. It was astounding how presumptuous she was.

"Actually, yes. People come here to mingle and to play. Not to spy on one another." She pursed her lips, studying me. "Some might say you are invading his privacy."

I looked down at my feet, then back up. I wanted to punch her, but instead decided to comply with her strange rules. "I understand. Checking someone out is not cool. I gotcha."

I decided to lay it on. "It's just that I have a fondness for watching. But I'll curb that." I tried to look contrite. "Thank you for letting me know this was not in the spirit of the club."

"You are welcome, B. You are always welcome." She finally left.

The woman was paranoid.

Although…she had good reason to be.

I headed toward G. There probably wasn't much to learn by watching him, and with M up my ass, I was just short of losing my shit.

There was another tap on my shoulder.

Jesus, what does that woman want?

But it wasn't M. It was the bartender.

"Hi." I continued toward G.

But the bartender moved faster, blocking my way. "Can I get you a drink? I'm done for the night."

"Thanks, but I have plans."

He grabbed my arm. And it wasn't a gentle grab. "Aw, c'mon. We can finish what we started."

He recognized me without my mask?

I pulled away, but his grip only tightened. What the hell? "Will you let me go?"

His brows furrowed. "Why?" He looked surprised.

"I am meeting a friend. I need you to let go of my arm. *Now.*"

But before he could release me, someone grabbed *his* arm.

He looked like he'd seen a ghost. "Oh! Mr. G, nice to see you this evening."

What a relief.

"I appreciate your keeping my friend company." G's voice was friendly. His expression was not.

"Yes, sir," the bartender said obediently. "Have yourselves a great evening." He disappeared into the crowd.

And *that* was how it was done.

"Thank you. I appreciate that."

"Glad I could help. I'll be talking to Miss M about her over-enthusiastic employee."

He led me by the hand to a loveseat at the edge of the room and I fell into its soft cushions.

"Thank you again for saving me over there. It was very gallant."

"Well, his grabbing your arm like that was bullshit. He'll be looking for another job soon enough."

This was my opportunity. "Speaking of Miss M, I don't think she likes me."

He laughed. "She's interesting, that one."

I persisted. "Earlier, she asked why I was looking at you and told me I shouldn't. It was very strange."

What was strange was talking to someone whose face I couldn't see.

"Well, *were* you looking at me?"

Busted.

"I guess. What's the big deal?"

He shrugged. "I don't see any harm in it. But she likes to keep everything under control and to her liking. I wouldn't worry about it."

He nodded to a couple walking by.

Now that we'd found each other, I had to get some info out of him. Every other inquiry I'd made had been met with a wall. I needed a new approach.

And I needed to move fast. M had a problem with me, and I didn't want to know what she did with problems.

CHAPTER 23

VARDEN

I slipped the Audi's gearshift into *park* outside Silk, and unlocked the glove box for my mask.

If it ever got out that I went to sex clubs—well, San Francisco was open-minded, but understanding only went so far.

So I was always careful. Very careful.

And I had to watch myself around Saffi, too.

Miss M greeted me, like she always did, with a kiss on my mask. I ran a soft finger down her bare arm, leaving goose bumps in its wake. Her usual steely look dissolved momentarily, and I could practically smell her need. She might be in a sex club night after night, but that didn't mean she was getting serviced.

Poor thing.

I wandered through the packed first floor, discreetly watching one couple take seats on a large sofa next to another man and woman. After some furtive glances, the two women began chatting, leading to introductions, and eventual laughter. It was just a matter of time before they retired to a room upstairs where the men would trade their eager wives, everyone excited at the prospect of some unfamiliar pussy and cock. I couldn't help but smile inside my mask.

Some couples played all the time, and for some, it was a once-in-a-lifetime adventure. They'd never forget their night at the club, that was for sure.

I grabbed myself a drink and cruised up to the second floor where the real partying took place. I spied my friends X, Y, and Z and decided to kill some time chatting them up while waiting for Saffi. Or B, as I'd be calling her.

It was fucking hot she had no idea who I was. And I planned to keep it that way.

"Well, look who it is! Mr. Mask." I couldn't be sure which woman was which, but did it really matter?

"Ladies. How are you, my beautiful alphabet girls?"

After a chorus of greetings, one leapt to her feet to get a fresh round of drinks. The curvy one patted a spot on the sofa for me to squeeze into. Once wedged between two of the beauties, one of them played with the edges of my mask.

This, I did not like, and gently removed her hand.

"Now, now. You know I don't remove my mask at the club."

"Aw, c'mon. You're so hot. I want to see more of you," she whined.

"Sweetie, that's not part of the deal."

She shrugged. "Can't blame a girl for trying."

"Hey," the other said, running a finger down the side of

my neck to my chest. "What do you say we go to one of the rooms?"

"Yes," the skinny one said. "How 'bout a little ménage?"

I stretched my arms along the back of the sofa, and reached around their shoulders.

"How 'bout you show me what you're talking about?" I drew them toward each other with a hand on each of their backs.

They leaned in at my invitation, their mouths close but not quite touching each other, perhaps contemplating what they might do to convince me to take them to a more private setting.

"Well. Look at you three." The third had returned with drinks.

She stood before us, clad in sheer lace panties, high heels, and glittery nipple tape on her perky breasts. Her mask was an ornate confection in all black with feathers shooting from the brow, like the plume on a quail.

Then she ran off to say hi to someone else, and the little bounce in her tits made my dick twitch.

Shit. Saffi. Where the hell was she?

"Ladies," I said, untangling myself from their limbs and standing. "I've got to move on."

They rolled their eyes.

"C'mon. Beauties like you never sit alone for long," I reassured them.

"All right then. Maybe next time?"

"Of course." I ran a finger down each of their cheeks. They were hotties, no doubt about it. But I had other plans for the night.

I surveyed the room, greeting people I knew as regulars, stopping to make small talk when I had to.

I planned to see Saffi before she saw me, which was entirely possible since few single women attended the club alone. She might not realize, it but she stood out like a store thumb. In a good way.

I made a lap around the second floor. Most of the playrooms had wide open doors regardless of what was going on inside. Only on the rare occasion did someone close or lock a door for privacy. I poked my head inside a couple of them, and while the scenes unfolding were damn exciting, none of them turned up my little reporter.

The last room I looked in had a literal pile of women going at it. I didn't want to intrude, seeing as there were no men there, but the play looked sweet. My cock stirred again, reminding me it would soon need some attention of its own.

Just inside the door, watching, was the woman in the half mask I'd seen the night before. She was stunning in her high heels, pencil skirt, and perfect hourglass shape.

Why did she seem so familiar?

She didn't notice me, so enthralled as she was with the scene playing out before her.

Hmmm.

I left to check out the third floor, the part of the club that saw the most action. It lacked the dance floor and bar the other floors had. People went up there for serious play. Or whatever suited their fancy.

But still, no Saffi.

So I broke down and texted her.

CHAPTER 24

VARDEN

J esus, she was beautiful. And intriguing. Innocent and earnest, but on another level sophisticated and sexy.

She probably hadn't been with a whole lot of guys. Maybe she'd had an older lover at some point who'd taken his time and taught her how to have some game. He'd probably been very patient, licked her pussy slowly and carefully, and opened her up like a flower—

"G...hello?"

"What? Oh yeah, sorry." Get with the program, asshole.

I threw an arm around her shoulders. "I have to tell you," I cut myself off *just* before calling her Saffi, "I've been thinking about you."

I seriously wanted to kiss those lips. But my goddamn mask...

"Thanks." She hid her face with a sip of her champagne.

"You are beautiful, B."

She didn't look up.

I hooked my finger under her chin. "You know that, don't you? That you are fucking beautiful?" My dick had been hard since I rescued her from the asshole bartender. I might as well go for it.

"You know how many times I've jacked myself while thinking of you?"

Holy shit! Those pretty cheeks were turning red now...and I could swear I got a whiff of sweet pussy from under her skirt.

"Oh. I'm sorry, I didn't mean to embarrass you," I said. "But that time on the stairs the other night was hot as hell..."

I let go of her face and hung my head. I had to go big since she couldn't read my expression.

"No need to apologize." She patted my arm.

"I have an idea. Let's go to one of the private rooms and get away from the crowd."

I stood and took her hand to help her up.

Damn if she wasn't nearly my height in her skyscraper heels. Her narrow pencil skirt hugged her hips to perfection, and her halter-top danced over her swinging breasts.

That's my girl. No bra.

I walked as best I could with my raging hard on, leading her by the hand to a room few knew about—and for which we paid dearly for the privilege.

"Wow. I didn't know this was back here," Saffi said.

Varden shut the door behind them. "Not many do."

The room's light came on soft, creating a boudoir-like atmosphere. I'd been here a few times before, but Saffi explored the room with an open mouth and wide eyes. She ran her hand over the velvet-flocked wallpaper, and circled to check out the huge, tri-fold mirror in one corner, and the satin settee and lounge chair in the other. She stopped in the center where two chairs clustered around a small table.

I hadn't played in a room like this in ages, probably because I hadn't been inspired. But I was now. Even if Saffi were the daughter of my attorney. Something about her...was beyond irresistible.

"You like it?" I asked.

"Like it? It's amazing. Gorgeous. It even smells nice," she said excitedly.

"Like you." I reached into a small chest of drawers and pulled out a long strip of silky fabric. Holding the fabric between two hands, I held it up to her.

"May I?"

She knit her brow. "Um. I'm not sure what you want to do, but I think I can guess..."

"I'd like to blindfold you. Then I'll take off my mask and kiss you."

Her face softened and she moved closer. "Oh!"

She was killing me with her big grin. I wouldn't have minded just tearing her clothes off right then and there.

Instead, I draped the silk over her eyes, tying its ends behind her head, careful not to catch her glossy hair.

"Comfortable?" I asked.

She reached up to adjust it. "Actually, yes."

I backed her up until her ass was planted on the room's table. I checked her blindfold one more time, and removed my mask.

Ahhh. Fresh air hit my face and it was heavenly. The mask served its purpose, but it could be a pain in the ass, too.

I leaned toward her to finally feel her lips. And they were as soft and delicious as I knew they'd be.

I brushed my lips against her mouth, as if to warm up, and she relaxed into the sensation with a small moan and shuddering breath. With a hand behind her head, I pressed more firmly and lips parted just enough to tickle her with my tongue. She leaned into me to increase the pressure and in a moment, I was pressing kisses all over her stunning face, even on the silk that covered her eyes.

I pulled her toward the edge of the table and pushed up her narrow skirt by slowly parting her knees, exploring until I gripped the back of her thighs, and then her juicy ass.

I looked down at her, legs spread wide open, skirt pushed up to her hips, and my god, she was wearing no panties. I spread my fingers, still gripping her behind, so that they fell into the crack of her ass cheeks. My fingers crept to the center of her cleft, sliding until they found her growing moisture. Her breath came deep and hard.

With her firmly in my grip, I returned to her mouth, licking, nibbling, teasing. Her knees spread wider and she squirmed against my hands.

"Baby," he whispered.

She continued grinding. "Yeah?"

"I'm gonna taste your pussy."

She shivered, her nipples poking through the thin fabric of her top.

I got to my knees, at last face-to-face with her clean-shaven pussy. I'd had my hand down there the other night, and I'd been thinking about burying my face in it since then. She smelled amazing, just like a woman, sexy and turned on.

Her lips were swollen with the excitement of watching people fucking and the knowledge that she was about to get fucked herself. I almost creamed myself right there when a few drops of her heavenly cum ran down her pink slit. I ran a finger through it and drew it right into my mouth.

"Fuck, baby. You're good."

I wet my finger with her juices again, this time bringing it up to her mouth.

"Open," I told her.

She accepted my finger, which she greedily sucked, enjoying her own tang and licking her lips like a hungry little animal.

"More," she murmured.

I smiled, not that she could see it, and my fingers returned to her pussy for more. This time, I paused at her opening.

But she, impatient, pushed her hips against my hand.

I slipped two fingers inside, making that "come here" motion to get her G spot.

"Oh god. Oh my god. Yes, like that," she murmured.

With the blindfold on, she reached for anything in front of her, and got a grip on my shirt, yanking until the buttons burst.

Christ. Wait till she had my cock in her.

I withdrew my fingers, stood her up, and spun her to face away.

"Bend over," I commanded, guiding her shoulders down to the table until she was bent at a ninety-degree angle.

There she stood in her high heels, creamy ass hanging out, pussy dripping cum onto the floor.

Holy shit.

CHAPTER 25

SAFFI

Christ, this guy was something. I'd forgotten all about work and the reason I was there to begin with. And I did not give a damn. Everything else was irrelevant.

All I knew was that I was in a sex club that nobody knew about with a man I'd met only once, bent over with my legs spread wide open.

I couldn't see a damn thing with the blindfold he put on me, but then I didn't need to. For some crazy reason I trusted him.

Was it that I finally got to experience his lips on mine? His kiss was strong but tender, and so massively sexy it left me lightheaded. And when they traveled south to my pussy, well, I nearly lost my mind.

Now I was bent over, and had a pretty good idea of what was coming.

Smack.

Okay, I wasn't expecting *that*.

He'd spanked my ass and god, it stung. But the pain dissolved when he smoothed his palm over my red-hot skin. When I was relaxing into his soothing touch, there came another.

Smack.

His slap fell on the other side of my ass, leaving me with watering eyes and a brand new burning pain that grew until he resolved it with the very same hand that had caused it.

I'd never been spanked, and the strange thrill of letting someone give me pain, then take it away, was dizzying. The power in it was staggering and I couldn't explain why, but it made me feel so close to this man whose face I'd never seen, and who I barely knew.

I squirmed to stand, but his hand in the middle of my back kept me down. I didn't mind.

"Relax, B."

His fingers slipped between my legs again, and ran up and down my slit. I gasped and arched my back, pushing into his strokes. While I tried to keep my thoughts straight, my breath grew ragged and I couldn't stop my head's bucking. In spite of being pinned, I forced my legs further open. I fell into an orgasm that crashed through me in powerful shudders, leaving me weak and only partly aware of where I was or who I was with.

Before I came down completely from my orgasm, G dragged some of my juice up to my asshole.

Oh god.

He ran his finger over my opening, prolonging the

shivers my climax had left me with. My toes curled inside my shoes and I pushed my ass higher for more.

I felt like a slut, and I goddamn loved it.

"You good, B? You like having your asshole played with?"

"Mmmm," was all I could manage.

"How do you like this?" His finger pushed inside me, and while I couldn't be sure how deep he went, I gasped from the painful burn.

"You okay?"

I could only nod. For some reason, I wanted more.

A drawer opened and closed and I could only guess he'd gotten ahold of some lube, because a warm moisture eased the friction of his finger. The burning subsided, replaced with a craving for more. He worked his finger deeper, pumping in and out, and joined it with another one.

Holy. Fucking. Shit.

I reached for my clit and worked it until I convulsed again in orgasm, writhing on the table with my ass full of his fingers.

Holy shit, I'd never felt anything like it.

Behind me, G's breath grew raspy and his groans louder as I realized he was stroking himself.

Suddenly, warm cum drenched the crack of my ass as he shot his load all over me.

"Fuck," he murmured.

His hot semen dribbled over my ass and down my thighs to mingle with my own juices. Christ, I was a mess.

"Stay there."

He'd gotten a towel, which he used to gently mop me

up. I was still blindfolded, but the room smelled of my perfume and our animal rut. With two hands, he helped me slowly straighten. He pulled my skirt down over my hips and led me to the settee where he embraced me as we both recovered.

"G?"

"Yeah?"

"Can I take the blindfold off?"

"You can. But first, I want to put my mask back on."

"Okay. Let's just relax then," I said.

"So tell me, B," he asked, "what brings you to the club?"

Uh-oh. I stiffened, hoping he didn't notice. "Oh, you know. Just wanted to see what it was all about."

Think fast.

"Why do *you* come here?" I asked.

"It's a respite from an otherwise stressful life."

He paused. "And it's a great equalizer. It doesn't matter who you are here or where you come from. Everyone is the same, they're here for the same reason, and they understand the rules. I don't really need to think. Just feel."

Well. I was speechless, never having expected him to really answer. And here *I* was deceiving him and everyone else at the club. The warm, sexy recovery I'd been enjoying withered, and the fact that I wasn't making much progress on my story bit me in the ass.

"Okay," he said. "Now you tell me something personal."

"I...I don't really have anything to share." I sprang out of his embrace and sat up. "I'd like to take off my blindfold. Is your mask nearby?"

I heard him get up, cross the room, and slide the mask

over his face. He came back and removed my blindfold. I had to blink to adjust to the light in the room, and there he was, with his mask back on.

"I need to head out," I said, standing.

I could only see the slits of his eyes through the mask, but it looked like something passed over them.

"Well then," he said, and finished putting himself back together.

I opened my purse and my mask jumped out. Fortunately G was trying to figure out how to button his jacket to cover the buttons I'd ripped off, and missed it.

I finger combed my hair and wiped on some lipstick. I didn't have to look perfect, but I didn't want to look freshly fucked, either. I headed for the door.

With my hand on the knob, I turned back to him. "Thank you. I had a very hot time."

He took a step toward me but stopped. "Can I walk you downstairs?"

I looked down at my high heels, then back up at him. My attraction to him was palpable, but my irritation with myself was even stronger. "If you don't mind, I'd like to see myself out. Good night."

"Good night, B."

I flew out the door, down the stairs, and blended into the crowd. The last thing I wanted was for him to watch me leave. Our physical compatibility was undeniable, and it was shitty to deceive him and use him for my story.

He would never know the important role he'd be playing in my reporting, and I planned to keep it that way. I could see it now: *The Man in the Venetian Mask...*

I might have just found my opening line.

CHAPTER 26

VARDEN

I gazed out my office's floor-to-ceiling windows, which overlooked San Francisco and the gorgeous Bay Bridge.

My admin had just brought my third cup of coffee for the morning. My late night drowsiness had been chased off by caffeine, only to be replaced by the jitters. And to be honest, some disappointment in the way Saffi had hit the road.

Crazy. Our "thing" could never go anywhere, anyway. And I was a shit for deceiving her. But on the other hand, I'd been able to come. I couldn't pretend that wasn't a big deal.

A knock sounded at my office door.

"Come in."

Our newest associate, an attractive young woman named Dani, walked in. She wore a snug dress outlining her curves and those high-heeled ankle boots that all the women seemed to be wearing. No wonder the younger guys in the office were going crazy over her.

"Dani. What can I do for you?"

"Well, Mr. Gallagher—"

"Dani, I told you to call me Varden."

She blushed. "Right. Varden." She approached my desk and gingerly touched its beveled edge.

"Did you need something?" The coffee jitters had given way to a pounding headache, leaving me in no mood for someone who couldn't get to the point.

"I did. I mean, I do. Need something," she said, looking down at the desk.

I waited.

She took a deep breath. "I need some help with the valuation of that new company we have coming in."

She finally looked at me. "I was wondering if we could work on it over drinks or dinner sometime this week."

Jesus Christ. Last thing I fucking needed.

"I'm happy to work with you on this, but we'll be sticking to office hours."

She walked around my desk to half-sit on the corner of it, parting her knees so I could see the top of her thigh highs, and...oh, shit. She wasn't wearing panties.

Was she really doing this? Really?

"What do you think?" she said softly.

It was all I could do to keep from kicking her the hell out.

"I gotta tell you right now, this is not gonna happen. I don't hook up with my employees. Ever." I stood to put some space between us.

She looked surprised. A beautiful woman unaccustomed to being told *no*. She crossed her arms. "Okay. That's fine. Then I'll quit."

"*What?*"

Was she insane?

"You heard me. I'll quit if that means I can sleep with you." She stuck her chin out.

"Actually"—I shook my head—"it does not mean anything of the sort." I had to admit, however, that her ballsiness was kind of hot.

I rose from my chair, and without turning my back on her, made my way to the office door. Pulling it open, I peeked out for my admin.

She was there, thank god. I sent her our secret signal— the okay sign— that said I needed saving. I'd used it in several instances over the years, although never for one quite like this.

She rushed right in and Dani popped off my desk, her skirt sliding back to its proper place.

"Dani," she exclaimed, heading straight for her with long, fast strides. "Someone was just walking down the hall, looking for you. I think I heard something about an urgent meeting?"

"Oh! On my way." Dani went running out of the office, her heels clicking down the hall until she could no longer be heard.

"Whew," I said. "Thank you. I owe ya."

"My pleasure. Is everything all right?" Her gray hair and glasses hanging from her neck reminded me of a librarian. She was the best admin anyone could ever want.

"Yeah. Do me a favor. Don't let her in here again unless it's with a group of people. She could be trouble.

And not the good kind of trouble if you know what I mean."

"Gotcha, boss." She smiled like the smooth diplomat she was and pulled the door closed behind her.

God bless that woman.

Not that I would *mind* fucking that little Dani senseless. But there just was no way I'd pull shit like that in the office. I'd worked too hard and wasn't about to blow it on some pussy. There was enough of it around I didn't need to look for it at work.

Which brought Saffi right back into my thoughts. And I was about to meet with her dad.

Christ.

As if on cue, my admin stuck her head back in my office. "You're ten a.m. is here, Varden."

"Thanks. Be right there."

I entered the crowded conference room and headed right for Hugh Bartlett. Saffi Bartlett's dad.

He shook my hand warmly.

"Hi, everyone," I said to the room. "Thanks for gathering this morning. Welcome to the office, Hugh. Good to see you."

"You, too, Varden."

The meeting came off without a hitch, and the analyses of some new potential investments were looking good. Very good.

After the room had cleared, I walked Hugh to the door. "Thanks for coming by this morning, Hugh."

"My pleasure," he said, smiling.

He should smile. He made a small fortune every time the firm made a new investment.

"Say," I asked, "how is your lovely daughter? What was her name? Saffi?"

Like I could forget the name of the woman I finger banged the night before...

Hugh's face lit up. "Oh, thanks for asking. She's doing great. Working on some big story, she tells me. Top secret." He patted me on the shoulder.

That didn't sound like Little League bullshit.

"Well, good for her."

Hugh nodded. "Yeah, hopefully this will help her move up the ladder, make a little more money. She's banking on her new story to be her break-out. Something about a club. A private country club or some such."

Fuck.

My stomach dropped and I leaned against the wall for support.

Breathe...

"What was that, Hugh?" I had to work to steady my voice. "Your daughter's doing a story about a club?"

He nodded proudly. "Yeah, sounds interesting, doesn't it? I can't wait to read it. The kid can write. Just like her mom."

He extended his hand. "Listen man, gotta run. Let's do dinner again soon, okay?"

"'Course."

As soon as he was gone, I rushed back to my office, slammed the door, and locked it.

"Varden?" My admin's voice rang from the other side of the door. "You okay?"

"Yup. Just a little headache."

Shit, shit, shit.

She wasn't doing a story on a *country* club. She was doing a story on a *fucking sex club*! How did I not figure that out? And I was probably going to be part of it.

I fell into my desk chair and buried my head in my hands.

I was pissed. Pissed at myself for doing anything that put me—and the firm—in harm's way.

I paced the office. Miss M had been right to be suspicious. Jesus, her instincts were good. I could learn a thing or two from her.

This is what happened when I let my dick lead me around.

Fuck, fuck, fuck.

'Course I couldn't be too furious. After all, wasn't I doing some deceiving, myself?

I had to get in touch with Saffi. If she knew who I was, she'd never reveal my identity.

Right?

CHAPTER 27

SAFFI

The Man in the Venetian Mask.

That looked damn good on paper.

Thanks, G, man of mystery. And sex god...

In the office the next morning, exhausted and drained by that insane session with my masked friend, I found myself on an unexpected roll. I sat at my computer and wrote for three hours straight. When the gang came by to give me their Chinese food order, I actually told them I was too busy.

God that felt good.

Tom invited himself into my cube.

"What?" I asked as I kept typing.

He frowned. "Saff, my friend. What're you so busy with? Heard you couldn't even get us lunch."

I whirled to face him. "Why don't you get your own goddamn lunch, Tom?"

His eyes widened and his head snapped back. "Damn.

Okay. I see how it is. Guess somebody's on her period. I'll leave you alone now. Although I did come over here to ask you something."

I pursed my lips in annoyance. *"What?"*

"Well, did you want to go out for a drink sometime after work?"

I was done.

"Get out of my goddamn cube. And if you ever talk about my period or anyone else's again, I will go right to HR."

He backed up, the color draining from his face.

I turned back to my writing after a couple deep breaths. I desperately needed to know more about the club—how long had it been around, how many members were there, how much money did it take in? And how did they keep the outside world from finding out about it? That would complete the story. And cement my reputation.

Just as I popped two aspirin, my editor, Ed, showed up at my desk.

"Saffi! You got a headache or something?" he asked.

I put on my "perky face" and looked at him. "Hey, Ed. I'm actually great. The story's coming along really well. I was just taking a break from writing."

That was only a little lie.

"Good. Good." He stood there, hands on hips, like he expected something.

So I jumped in with small talk. "You having a good day?"

"Oh yeah. Great day."

We kept looking at each other.

"Saffi, do you have something I could take a look at yet? Get a sense of how the story is coming together?"

Shit. I was afraid of that. "Yeah, sure. I mean... Well, can I have some more time with it first? I need to get a little more info about the club itself. It hasn't proved easy to do that."

"I can imagine. But I want something by end of the week. Okay?"

"Sounds good. Thanks, Ed."

Whew. That was a close one. Now, how was I going to finish the damn story?

And was I going to see G again?

As if he'd read my mind, a text popped up on my phone.

club? tonight?

Maybe he'd be the ticket to the info I needed. *If* I could get him to talk. And other things...

yes. 9:00?

c u then

Okay. That was taken care of.

I dialed my dad.

"Hey sweetie," he answered.

"Hey, Dad. I'm going out after work tonight, so don't wait on me for dinner."

"Okay. Hey, I saw my client, Varden, in a meeting this morning. You remember him?"

Wasn't he that good-looking guy from dinner? "Yeah, I

159

remember him. He seemed distracted by some ladies at the bar."

My dad laughed. "Well, he is a bit of a ladies' man. Anyway, he asked for you. I thought that was nice."

I made that much of an impression? "Really? He barely spoke to me that night."

"Well, he seemed to remember you fondly."

"That's nice. Anyway, I'll probably see you in the morning then, okay?"

"Sounds good. Love you."

Next, I phoned Nelle.

"Hey there," she answered.

"Hi. Got time for a drink after work?"

"Sure! See you at six?" she suggested.

"Awesome. See you then."

I needed to see Nelle, but first had to clear my head. I headed to the mailroom for a long walk.

This time, Nelle beat me to the bar. It was a first. I threw my arms around her.

"Dang, girl! You almost knocked me off my chair," she said. "Are you okay? What's up with the dramatic hug?"

Was my neediness that obvious?

"Oh gosh, sorry. I'm just so glad to see you." I waved the bartender over so I could join her in a beer.

"Well," Nelle started, "I'm off to London next week for work. I'm psyched."

"Oh my god, that sounds so glam."

She giggled. "It sort of does, doesn't it?"

"Hey, whatever happened with your office crush? The one who asked you out?" I asked.

She pursed her lips. "Ugh. He was a dick. We went to dinner. He had bad manners, was boring, and then was pissed I wouldn't let him up to my apartment at the end of the night."

"Oh, yuck. Well, glad it didn't go anywhere. You don't want to get involved with someone you work with, anyway."

"You're right. It could have been a freaking mess. Crisis averted," she said, dramatically swiping her hand across her forehead. "And what's up with your job?"

I hesitated, but I was desperate to talk. "That's pretty much why I wanted to see you tonight."

Her eyes opened wide. "No! Did you sleep with that guy in the office? And now everything's fucked up?"

"No, I did no such thing."

Disappointment washed over her face. She always loved a drama.

"What I have to tell you is way better," I teased.

Her disappointment was replaced with glee. "Ohmygod! Tell me." She slid to the edge of her seat.

"So...I told you I lined up a good assignment, something I hoped would really kick start my career and earn me some respect at the office."

"Yeah. I remember."

I took a sip of my beer. "I'm doing an undercover investigation."

"Get. Out." She cuffed me on the shoulder.

"It's true. And I want to tell you about it, but you've got

to keep this top secret and confidential. You cannot tell a soul until the story comes out."

"Promise, I promise." She did the whole *cross my heart* motion.

"Have you ever heard of Club Silk?"

She ran her hands through her hair while she thought. "You know, I have. Wasn't there some story in the news a few years ago that it was some secret sex club, but every time it was discovered, they moved it to another location?"

I nodded.

Her eyes bugged out of her head. She looked around and whispered, "You're doing a story on a sex club? Holy shit, tell me everything! Have you been there?"

I nodded.

"Was everyone just fucking with abandon, right there in public?"

"Pretty much. I mean, that's what goes on there, basically."

"Oh my god. Did you hook up with anyone?"

"I knew you were going to ask that." I laughed. "Yeah, there's a guy there who I've played with a couple times."

"So that's the term? *Play with?* I like it! Now tell me about him."

"Well. He's very sexy. Kind of commanding, which I like. A lot."

She looked like she was going to explode. "Is he hot? What's he look like?"

Some things were going to be hard to explain. "I don't exactly know."

"*What?*"

"I know that sounds crazy, but I don't know. He wears a mask."

She grimaced. "Okay, that is creepy. Really weird. He must be ugly. Not sure I'd be down with that."

"I suppose he could be ugly. He says he wears it to protect his privacy. Whatever that means. Anyway, it's been quite the experience. It's also a mysterious place."

"Yeah? How so?"

I leaned closer to her. "When I ask questions—really basic stuff like how long the club's been around, how many members it has, etc.—no one will answer them. It's the weirdest thing."

Nelle put her elbow on the bar and propped her chin on it, her brow furrowed.

"Do you think it's safe to go sniffing around there for info? Don't you think you should leave well enough alone?"

"I feel safe, I mean I've been pretty discreet. But without some background on the club, I don't have a well-rounded story."

In truth, the story wasn't the only reason to go back. The masked man had been intruding on my thoughts all day long. And left an ache between my legs.

"Just be careful, okay?" She grabbed my arm. "I'm serious. Don't take any chances. But I do think it's super cool you're going to a sex club."

"Shhh. You don't have to *announce* it." I looked around the bar.

She clapped her hands. "So, what's it like? C'mon, tell me."

I lowered my voice further. "At first it's jarring to see

people fucking in public. But once you get beyond that, it's hot. I mean, it's a real turn-on, actually."

"After I come back from London, will you take me there?" she begged.

"I'm not sure, I'll see. I mean, once my story comes out, they may never let me in again."

"Right. Enjoy it while you can." She threw her head back and laughed.

"My little friend, Saffi. Sex goddess."

Actually, I did feel like a sex goddess, thanks to G.

Nothing wrong with that.

CHAPTER 28

VARDEN

I got to the club well before nine to make sure I had time to scope the place out before Saffi arrived.

Now that I knew her real reason for coming, I had to admit I vacillated between anger and intrigue. She was no wimp, that was for sure. She was going for it. And reaping a few benefits while she was at it.

"G! I'm so glad you could join us tonight," M said. She was poured into a slinky red number that stood out like a beacon in the sea of mostly black-clothed club-goers.

"M. Stunning as always." Her nipples strained against the silk of her dress, but strangely, I didn't feel anything beyond admiration—there was just no attraction.

M hooked her arm in mine like we were best friends, and led me from the crowd to a private corner.

What was she up to?

"G." She looked very intently into my eyes. After all, it was all she could see of my face.

"I've noticed you playing with a new member of ours. B? I asked you about her before."

"Yes, we have been playing together. But I really don't know anything about her. If you're looking for info you'll have to ask her yourself."

I was not about to share what I'd learned. No freaking way. And M did not look happy with me.

She continued. "I don't know about her. Something doesn't seem right. I may ask her to leave the club."

I shrugged, trying to play it cool. "She seems okay to me."

"I need to find out who she is and what she's doing here. You won't help?" she asked.

"I don't know. I wouldn't want anyone in my business, so why would I pry into someone else's?" asked in return.

Frustration crossed her face.

"This is not the same, and you know it. This is about the safety of our club, ensuring its longevity. We all need to be vigilant."

What a shit show.

How was I going to tell Saffi that M was on to her when I wasn't supposed to know who the hell she was?

"I'll see what I can do," I told her.

She smiled demurely and gushed, "I knew I could count on you. Thank you, G."

She planted a light kiss on the side of my mask, the closest she'd ever get to my bare face.

It all made sense, now. Saffi had probably thought she'd been plenty discreet, but really had no idea what the hell she was getting into. Women rarely came to the club alone, and when they did, they didn't wander around asking questions. The ones who did were asked not to return.

No wonder M's suspicions were raised.

Then why was M still letting Saffi come around?

Maybe because of me. M knew I'd taken a liking to her.

Things were getting complicated. What would M do if she found out Saffi was not only a reporter, but also doing a story on her beloved club?

With the evening young, I went up to the second floor and found an empty playroom. I locked the door and took a seat, removing my mask. I had to find a way to clue Saffi in. Shit. Things had gone too far. And with the daughter of a business associate, no less.

Initially, going after Hugh's super hot, off-limits daughter had been a rush. But it wasn't a game anymore. Not for Saffi, and not for me.

I had to talk to her, tell her what was up. There was just no way around it. Even if it meant revealing my identity.

I replaced my mask and ventured back into the club. In the few minutes I'd been hiding out, the place had transformed into a party in full swing. From my vantage point on the stairs leading down to the main floor, I spotted Saffi just coming in. Miss M had also noticed her and was beelining through the crowd toward her. I ran down the stairs and pushed through the crowd. I had to reach her first.

I caught them just in time for M to invite Saffi to her office for a "talk." There was no telling what she was up to, nor why she had to speak to Saffi in private, but I quickly inserted myself.

"Hey beautiful." I put an arm around Saffi and pulled her to me.

But M did not give up so easily. She put her hand on my arm. "Excuse me, G. We were just going to have a little chat."

She stared at me with a strange intensity.

"Oh, M, I know you don't want to deny me the pleasure of my friend's company. Your chat can wait till later, can't it?"

M looked like someone had gravely insulted her. And yet her smile never wavered. It was as if nothing could break through that veneer of perfect composure. The dark annoyance existed only in and around her eyes.

M generously placed an arm around the shoulder of each of us. "You two go have fun. This promises to be a great night." She blew us a kiss and disappeared into the crowd.

I vowed to keep Saffi within my sights. And when I took a good look at her, I could think of nothing more that I wanted. How the hell did she get out of her father's house looking as gorgeous as she did?

Her dark red sleeveless dress was made of some slinky

material that swirled around her curves as she moved. Her high-heeled pumps must have been five inches. Part of her dark hair was pulled behind her head, and the rest of it tumbled down her back in long waves. Her lips were infinitely kissable, and for the first time in a long time, I was irritated my mask stood between me and her soft skin.

I extended my arm for her to take and leaned toward her ear. "You look amazing."

Her smile startled me. How was it she was more gorgeous every time I saw her? How was that even possible?

"Well, you don't look too bad yourself." She laughed, running a finger down the side of my mask. She tilted her head and considered me.

I shook my finger at her. "I know what you're thinking. Don't even try."

She laughed.

"The mask stays on," I told her.

She gave a good-natured shrug. "Okay, my mysterious friend."

We approached the stairway to the second floor.

"So what's on the agenda tonight, G?" she asked flirtatiously. Seemed like she was getting more comfortable with the place. And me.

"Well," I said as we climbed the steps. "I have ideas. But what about you?"

She took my hand, surprising the hell out of me, especially after the way she took off last time. "I have an idea or two."

I led her to the quietest spot available—a small, empty

loveseat in a semi-dark corner. I got her champagne and for myself, the usual.

After a long draw on her bubbly, she settled into the seat's cushions. "I'm starting to see some familiar faces now that I've been here a few times. I wonder how many members there are."

She looked around the mezzanine and turned to me as if expecting an answer.

Now that I knew she wasn't a pain in the ass, but just trying to get ahead at work, I felt for her and for some crazy reason was driven to help. She wasn't likely to learn much more about the club than what she could gather with her own eyes. Her inquiries were drawing attention —and not the good kind.

She waved her hand to encompass the whole room. "Would you happen to know?"

I shrugged.

"Why is this place so secretive? I just don't get it."

"C'mon. Can you seriously ask that question?" I said.

She raised her eyebrows. "Why not? What's wrong with being curious?"

Was she really that naïve?

"Sa—silly girl." Shit, I'd almost slipped. "Those of us who come here want our privacy protected."

"So the thought is that if you don't ask questions, no one will ask you questions back?"

"Now you're getting it." I patted her head.

She laughed.

I looked her up and down, and damn if her tits didn't hang just right under that silky fabric. She had the perfect rack for going braless, and I couldn't wait much longer to get my hands on her.

I wanted to help her, but I wanted to protect my privacy a lot more.

CHAPTER 29

SAFFI

Ugh.

G still refused to fork over even a bit of information about the club.

Who knew this would be so hard? What a lesson learned. To have thought I could just waltz in and uncover all the club's secrets to share with the world. What the hell had I been thinking? No wonder Ed had been on my ass for a draft. He didn't believe I could do this.

And now I was beginning to wonder if I could, too.

But I wasn't going to dwell on that. I couldn't give up yet. I was in the company of the sexy and mysterious G, and even with his blasted mask, he still got my panties wet. God, what if he was hideous behind that thing?

Well, it's not like I was going to marry him.

He reached for my erect nipple, straining against the clingy jersey of my dress. Scooping just inside the low neckline, he pushed the stretchy fabric out of the way. When he made contact with my flesh, his fingers tightened just until the pain became too much, as if he could read my mind.

I dropped my head, savoring the tingling that shot from my breast straight to my core.

His other hand reached for my cheek and stroked it slowly. As his hand wandered along my jaw, his other one grabbed a fistful of my hair and held it tight.

"You wanna play with me, little girl?" he growled.

The power in his voice sent me to an unfamiliar place, one that was scary and exhilarating. Paralyzed with an aching lust, all thoughts aside from being ravished fled my mind. It was disorienting, and yet I knew exactly what I wanted.

I pushed his hands away, causing him to stiffen. Unable to see his face, it was the only way I could read him. But I didn't care. He'd be very happy in a few short moments.

I left the couch to drop to my knees. He relaxed back on the sofa to watch me fumble with his belt and fly, and finally free his hard cock to enjoy for the first time.

A drop of precum hung from its tip. I ran my finger to scoop it up to my lips. With closed eyes, I savored his salty essence, sliding my finger in and out of my mouth with his gaze locked on me.

My fingers, grasping his erection, were unable to fit around its circumference, and when I reached the swollen head, my grip had to open considerably.

I pushed between his legs to lower my mouth on him. At first, I took only enough of the head to taste him and get the crown wet. When he growled and threw his head back, I engulfed him with my mouth, his length sinking to the back of my throat. He released a laugh, followed by a holler.

"Shit, shit, shit," he said, banging his head against the sofa.

I continued pistoning with my mouth, taking his balls in hand and twisting them gently. With my free hand I reached back between my legs to pull up my dress and begin working my clit.

G thrust his cock into my mouth as if I might be able to take him deeper. With a hand on top of my head, he pushed until I gagged.

He started to explode.

I thought I'd died and gone to heaven.

"Fuck, fuck, fuck, I'm coming," he bellowed.

I continued to suck until his cum slammed against the back of my throat. I gulped it quickly so I could take more.

When I'd swallowed it all, I slid off his softening length and rested my head on his thigh. He stroked my hair, then took me by the arms and pulled me into his lap.

"You are really something, my beautiful B. Maybe someday, you'll tell me your real name."

"Maybe I will," I said, "if you'll let me see your face."

He laughed. "Fair enough. We'll see, beautiful, we'll see."

I slid from his lap to rearrange my disheveled clothes. He straightened out his own shirttails and tucked himself back into his pants.

"You know, B," he said, "you ask questions, and yet I know nothing about you."

"I thought you were the one just lecturing about privacy."

"You're right. I did. But that didn't stop you from asking."

I shrugged. "I'm just naturally curious."

"Okay. I'm curious, too. What do you do for work?" he asked.

Oh shit. Was he suspicious?

"I'm a writer."

"A writer," he exclaimed. "Now that's interesting."

Shit. Here come the questions. Time to exit.

"Tell me what you write."

"Oh, all sorts of things. But hey, I don't want to talk about this now. In fact, I'm tired and I have to get up early." With some reluctance, I stood.

"Oh, I'm sorry to hear that."

Was he? Or was I just a booty call?

"Walk me to the door?" I extended my hand.

Before I could lead him downstairs, he surprised me by stopping, holding my arms, and looking at me intently. It was the most uncomfortable stare I'd ever experienced, and yet I couldn't tear myself away. It was also the closest I'd been to his masked face, and in the dim light, I saw flecks of blue in his otherwise dark eyes.

It wasn't fair. I needed to see his face.

"I want see you again, B." His demanding tone reignited the throbbing in my sex.

My gaze shifted over his shoulder, and I saw M

watching us from across the room. Our eyes met, and I quickly turned back. "I think we might be able to arrange that. Hey, can I ask you a question?"

"Nothing's ever stopped you before."

With my chin, I gestured in the direction of the watchful Miss M, now talking to some guests but with an eye on us.

"What is M's issue with me? Do you have any idea?"

I could have sworn he twitched when I asked, but I couldn't be sure. Glancing over his shoulder, he nodded to her in greeting.

"Um, I didn't notice. Are you sure?" he asked, turning back.

Of course he'd noticed. It was impossible not to.

But no sense in being confrontational. I wanted to see him again and not just to get more info for the story. "Maybe I'm imagining things."

On our way down the stairs, we stepped around a woman seated on the wide staircase. Before her was an enthusiastic man with his head between her legs, his mouth burrowing into her pussy. He held his exposed cock in a free hand.

Just as we stepped around them, the woman's legs began to shudder. Her chest heaved and she screamed, exploding in orgasm. The guy's hand pistoned over his dick and he shifted to shoot his load on the woman's glistening pussy.

Damn. There was something about watching other people fuck that was beyond arousing, as if I were right in the middle of their play. I swore I could sense that woman's ecstasy as she exploded. *Almost* as good as the real thing.

If I ended up being banned from the club, which could happen once my story was published—if it ever was published—I'd miss the place, for sure. I took one more glance around and actually felt a little sad.

With G's hand on the small of my back, we maneuvered through the good-looking crowd, busy flirting with each other and making new friends.

It was no surprise when M suddenly appeared in front of us.

"Hello M," G said, wrapping an arm around my waist.

If I hadn't known better, I'd swear he was being protective.

A benevolent smile spread across her face. She looked right at me as if G weren't there.

"You're not leaving, are you?" she said to me. "The night is young."

She placed a hand on my arm. Perhaps too firmly.

I shook it off.

"Our friend, B, has an early morning planned. She's heading out now," G said as we turned to maneuver around her.

But she stepped in our way, continuing to ignore him. "B, before you leave, do you have a moment to chat in my office?"

"She's leaving now." G pushed me toward the door.

M was trying to keep me, G was trying to rush me out. I wasn't sure what was going on, but there was no doubt I just wanted to leave.

I looked from one to the other. "I *am* leaving now. Hope to see you both soon."

I bolted for the door, taking a look back before it slammed shut. G's arms were crossed, and M leaned toward him with narrow eyes but an angelic smile, whispering.

I ran to my car and locked my doors.

CHAPTER 30

VARDEN

Thank god I'd been there to keep M from sinking her long and vicious claws into Saffi—who knew what that crazy witch could do.

My gut told me not to trust her. And my gut was nearly always right.

M turned to me after Saffi ran out the door, daggers in her eyes. "I needed to speak with her," she spat, trying to see my eyes beyond the mask.

I placed a hand on her arm to calm her. "She has an early morning, like I told you."

"I heard you." She turned to walk away, but before she could, I grabbed her arm.

"What did you need to talk to her about so urgently? What couldn't wait for another time?" I knew the answer but wanted her to say it.

"You know why I wanted to talk to her. I want to find out more about her. Figure out who she is, and why she's coming here. Something about her is not on the up-and-up."

"Would you relax? She comes here to get off, like everyone else does," I lied. "And now, I hope she's coming here to see me."

"*Thanks* for doing your part to keep the club safe from the wrong people."

She turned on her heel and left me standing there in the midst of the revelers.

Whoa.

My head was reeling and the mask was suddenly blistering hot—hotter than normal. It was all I could do to keep from tearing it off. An enthusiastic couple running for a private room slammed into me, leaving me teetering and careening into others. No one took notice as I fought to regain my balance.

When had the place become so crowded?

I struggled for long, deep breaths in the noisy overheated room and pushed for the door, ignoring greetings from other guests. Bursting into the cool, San Francisco night, I was relieved to find the street in front of the club empty and quiet. I ripped at my mask to gulp some fresh air and ran for my car.

I was done with that place for the night and since it was early yet, I called my brother to see if he wanted to go for a bite to eat.

On the short drive home I thought back to our younger days, before we could legally drink, when we'd go out for a beer at the local dive that wasn't concerned about serving minors. Even back then, one or two brews would turn into ten or a dozen for Beau.

That was the beginning of the end for him, and his life hadn't been the same since. For him, a beer once in a while turned into every night of the week, and several years on, I'd lost track of the number of times I'd put him in rehab, only to have him backslide.

And yet, I'd never give up on him. Never.

"Beau! Watcha doin?" I called as I came through the front door.

"Whattup, bro?" Beau asked as he met me. "I just finished an online meeting with my AA sponsor."

The puffiness that had consumed his face just a few days earlier had subsided, and I could swear there was a lightness in his step that hadn't been there in a long, long time.

"Wanna walk to that place around the corner?" I asked.

"Let's do it."

A few minutes later, we settled into a booth in the back corner of a neighborhood place and ordered from a pretty young waitress. I watched Beau's gaze follow her as she walked away.

"So. You're doing well. I'm proud of you."

He nodded. "Thanks, man. I don't know where I'd be with out you."

Shaking his head, his gaze settled on the placemat before him.

The waitress dropped off two non-alcoholic beers. I hated them but always drank them with Beau. Brotherly solidarity and all that.

"So, Var. How are *you*? I see you working hard and going out. You meeting any nice girls?"

I sipped my fake beer. "You know me. I like to fly solo.

But, there is this one woman I met not long ago. I'm kind of into her."

"Yeah? Way to go. Keep up the good work."

Yeah. She *was* proving to be some work, that was for sure. Her involvement in the club, and my involvement with her dad created a level of complication I usually ran from.

But not this time.

CHAPTER 31

SAFFI

Nelle was back from London, and I was desperate to talk to her. After a miserable day working on my Club Silk story, knowing full well I didn't have all the details I needed and that I'd probably never get them, I needed a shoulder to cry on. I arrived early at the bar where we always met and dove into my first beer.

"Heyyyyyy!" Nelle exclaimed, running into the bar with open arms and throwing them around me.

"I am *so* glad you're back," I said.

"Well, *I'm* not glad to be home. I freaking *loved* London and cannot wait to return. We have to go there, Saffi. It's the most amazing city."

She frantically waved over the bartender. "And the guys' accents are so hot. Oh my god. I am *so* marrying an Englishman."

I was chomping at the bit to discuss all that was on my

mind, but just listened. If I waited long enough, she'd run out of gas.

And she did, chattering on for five more minutes before slowing.

"So, Saff. What's up with you and the big story?" She leaned close to whisper. "And the sex club."

"Glad you asked," I said with patience. "I've hit some roadblocks. I think the club owner might be on to me."

Nelle's hand flew to her chest. "No way. Jesus. What will they do? I mean, could this be dangerous?"

"No," I said, wishing I believed my lie.

"The problem," I continued, "is that I'm having trouble finishing the story. Everyone there is tight-lipped and I haven't been able to get even the most basic info. I can probably finish the story, but it won't be that good."

"Aw c'mon. There's got to be a way. Won't anyone there talk?" she asked.

"You would think. But it's like they've been freaking programmed. They're the Stepford Wives of sex clubs."

"What about the guy you've been playing with? What's up with him?"

"He won't tell me anything, either. But I am kind of into him. It's the strangest thing. I don't even know what his face looks like."

Nelle frowned. "Yeah...that's kind of creepy."

I shook my head. "Oddly... I don't really care what he looks like. I'm so drawn to him, and I think he might feel the same way about me. It would be nice if he were hand-some, but it really doesn't matter."

She held her hands up in surrender. "All right...whatever." She pulled out her credit card and waved for the bill.

"I gotta run. This was my treat," she said.

"Where you going?" I asked.

"Got a conference call."

"What? So late?"

"Yeah. It's morning in Hong Kong, so we do our calls with them in the evening."

She was doing business with the Chinese, and all I ever did was go for takeout.

She air-kissed me and was gone.

I was taking the last swig of my beer when my phone vibrated with a message from G.

Hmmm. I swiped it phone open.

r u busy? meet me at four seasons bar for a drink?

Um, what?

What was that all about? He couldn't very well wear his mask at the Four Seasons. This was big. Something was up.

ok. what time?

in 15?

u wearing mask?

LOL. nope

how will I know u?

I'll know u

c u then

Holy shit, I was finally going to see his face. Would he have dimples? No, he didn't seem the dimple type. Would his lips be thin or full? Probably thin. Would his nose be straight or crooked? Best guess, crooked, but only slightly, from a fight as a kid.

I ran to the bathroom to smear on some glossy red lipstick and fluff my hair. I hustled over to The Four Seasons.

The cavernous hotel bar, dark and masculine with wood paneling, was quiet. Other patrons were scattered about, but it had been designed so that nothing more than whispers and the occasional laugh drifted through the air.

Settling into my second bar of the evening, I ordered a fancy cocktail and began texting Nelle about this latest development.

There was a tap on my shoulder, and I spun to my left.

"Saffi."

Oh.

It was my dad's client...the one who'd asked about me. Varden. What was he doing here?

"Hi. How are you?" I kept looking around the bar for G. He was five minutes late.

"Good. You?" he asked.

I turned back to him with a polite smile. "Nice to see you."

I kept looking around for G. Normally I would have been happy to chat with one of my father's clients. But now was not the time.

"What are you drinking there?" Varden asked.

"Um. It's a negroni."

"You look distracted," he said.

I glanced toward the door again, but the man entering was too old and short to be G.

"I'm sorry to be rude," I said to him. "But I'm expecting a friend. I do hope you have a good evening."

His expression changed. Was that amusement?

"I'll tell my dad you said hi," I added, hoping he'd take the hint. I felt kind of bad—he did seem nice and *was* damn good-looking.

I was on the edge of my seat waiting, but Varden just stood there. He seemed to have no intention of leaving.

God, why doesn't he take the hint?

Where was G? I reached for my phone and sent a text.

ur late. still coming?

I looked up from my phone.

Still Varden.

Shit.

"Varden, I'm really sorry but I have other plans tonight."

"I know you do, Saffi."

Huh?

"I know, because you made them with me," he said.

"What? What are you talking about?" I craned my neck toward the door. G could rescue me from an unwanted conversation like this.

"Saffi, I am G. From the club."

What. The. Fuck.

"How do you know about the club?" I was confused, but my stomach sank as if it knew something I wasn't ready to acknowledge.

He slid onto the barstool next to mine.

"We need to talk. I wear a mask at the club to protect my privacy," he said, looking at me intently.

Just like G would.

"But I wanted you to know who I really was, so I asked you to meet me here. We have something important to talk about."

He ordered bourbon. G always ordered bourbon.

A slow realization washed over me. My hand shook so much, my drink sloshed out of its glass.

"I…I don't believe you. Who put you up to this?" I swallowed hard to hide my shaking voice.

"I can prove to you that we've been at the club together."

No, no, no, no, no.

"I really don't think this is funny." Tears threatened to fill my eyes.

Get it together, girl.

The bartender brought Varden's bourbon. "Last time we were there, you wore a slinky dress with no bra and high heels. Your hair was partially pulled back. Miss M tried really hard to get you to her office, but I intervened."

G was also my father's client, Varden, and the man I'd met at dinner? I'd been intimate with an associate of my father's?

Please. It can't be so.

Tears distorted my vision, followed by spots of white light, and my heart pounded in panic.

"We got, uh…*intimate* on the second floor on one of the sofas. It was amazing—"

"*Shut up!*" I screamed.

The bartender's gaze snapped my way, and he headed over.

Confusion had me seconds away from vomiting right then. I reached for my cocktail, not sure why, because the last thing I felt like doing was consuming more alcohol. But my fingers slipped on the wet glass, causing it to tip and release my sticky drink all over the bar.

Varden put his hand on my arm. "I'm so sorry you're upset. When I first saw you at the club, I thought we'd do a little harmless messing around, but...I don't know...I found myself wanting to see more of you. And not just at the club."

He looked around as the bartender arrived. He leaned next to my ear. "I want to see you outside the club, here in the real world. In my real world. And yours."

"Miss, are you okay?" the bartender asked.

"Yes, thank you. I'll be fine."

I slid off my barstool, stepping away from Varden, but he only moved toward me.

"I'm sorry," he said.

The disappointment washed over me like acid, causing searing pain.

"How could you?" I mumbled. My eyes filled with tears despite my effort to deny them. The disappointment —the goddamn disappointment—that someone I'd begun to fall for had taken me for such a fool.

I *was* a fool. A huge fucking fool. To think I could write a superstar story for the Post, and attract some mysterious and sexy man at the same time.

Fucking idiot. That's me.

I hightailed it out of the Four Seasons. God I hoped I never saw G, or Varden, or whatever the hell his name was, again.

CHAPTER 32

VARDEN

Seeing how fucking devastated Saffi was at finding out who I really was—well, that was one of the low points of my life.

And there had been a lot of low points.

I'd thought she'd be annoyed. Maybe even pissed. But not hysterical with pain at my deceit.

She hated me. And in that moment, I hated myself.

She ran out of the bar, and for a second I thought I owed it to her *not* to follow. But I ran after her, anyway, grabbing her arm as soon as we hit the hotel lobby. I didn't want to attract the attention of hotel security or the well-heeled guests going about their business, but if I didn't get her to calm down quickly, we'd be creating a scene that wasn't going to be pretty.

"Saffi, dammit, would you wait just a minute?" I said.

She whirled around and tried to shake free. "Let go of me," she hissed, tears flowing.

"I need to tell you something very important. Please, just listen. It's for your own safety. After I'm done, if you want to take off, that's fine," I pleaded. "I wouldn't blame you at all if you did. My not telling you who I was when I knew your identity was a shitty thing to do."

"No kidding, you asshole. And why did you do it, then? Ugh, and to think you're my father's business associate." She looked at the floor, shoulders shaking.

"Please, Saffi. Just sit here with me. I need five minutes." I tilted my head toward the lobby's only unoccupied seating area.

"Five minutes."

"C'mon." I led her to a chair and sat directly opposite her.

She looked at me impatiently.

"Saffi, I had a meeting with your dad recently, and he mentioned you're working on an undercover story for the paper. I immediately figured out it was Club Silk."

The color drained from her face. "You didn't tell him anything about the club, did you?"

"No. God, no. I think he thinks you're investigating a country club or something. And he has no idea we've been…together. Anyway, I was immediately concerned about protecting my own privacy." I looked around the hotel lobby. "I have a lot at stake. But you know that."

"I'm not surprised. Thinking of yourself and no one else," she snapped.

She hadn't exactly been honest, either, but I would get to that.

"Then it became clear to me that M was on to you, suspicious about something."

"What did you tell her?" she hissed.

"Hold on. Jesus, I didn't tell her a thing."

She narrowed her eyes at me. I never would have guessed she was so full of fire.

"You didn't?" she asked.

"Are you kidding? Give me some fucking credit. I wasn't going to let her know I knew you or what you were up to. But listen. She's kept after me, asking me questions, demanding I get info. It's fucking crazy."

"What did you tell her?"

"That I knew nothing about you. I lied."

"How do I know you didn't give me away to her?" she asked.

"You'd know. For one, she wouldn't let you get near the place. But for another...well, she knows a lot of people."

She looked confused. Was she really that naive?

"And the people she knows, they're not all particularly...nice."

The color drained from her face as her expression shifted from anger to the unsteadiness of fear.

"She's suspicious of you. Look, she couldn't successfully run a club like Silk for as long as she has without a good sense of people. The point is, she doesn't know what you're up to. But I'm afraid she'll push till she finds out."

Saffi looked at her watch. "Thank you for the information." She stood to leave.

I held up a hand. "Wait, I'm not done."

"What?" She parked her hands on her hips.

"First of all, you have not been so honest yourself. You knew I was interested in you."

She looked down for a moment, the defiance draining from her face. "That's true, but—"

"Look, forget it. What I have to ask you is far more important. I'm not sure I have the right to, but I will anyway. I don't want it getting out that I've been anywhere near the club. Can I count on you for that?"

"If you wanted your identity protected, why did you reveal yourself?"

"I did it for you. Otherwise, you might not have listened to my warning."

She pulled her trench coat tight. "For all M knows, I go there to hook up. She can't prove anything."

"I'm gonna ask you again. Will you keep me out of your story?" I asked.

She'd started to walk away, but turned around quickly. "I don't know. I'll get back to you on that."

She gave a small laugh that was pissed off and sad at the same time. Then she was gone, leaving me in the middle of the Four Seasons lobby, full of shame like I hadn't experienced in a long time.

CHAPTER 33

SAFFI

Devastated.

I was fucking devastated.

But really—should I have been so surprised? What did I think was going to happen, meeting a guy at a sex club? It wasn't like he was gonna be a Boy Scout, for Christ's sake.

But Dad's freaking client?

I was pissed, sure. But the disappointment was what had its fingers around my heart, and it was squeezing. Hard.

Yeah, I'd taken a liking to G, or whatever the hell his name was. And I felt stupid. Goddamn stupid. And humiliated. The whole time he was probably getting off knowing he was pulling one over on his attorney's daughter.

Right?

But I had to wonder, if he didn't give a shit about me,

would he have revealed his identity to project me from M?

Those were questions I'd deal with later.

For now, what was I going to do with my story? I wasn't so sure Ed would accept it with what I had.

Fuck. Just fuck, fuck, fuck.

I ran for the cab waiting in front of the hotel. On the ride home, I pressed my temple against the cool car window. How did I get in such a predicament? A shitty job, where the most exciting thing I did most days was go to the mailroom and pick up lunch. A boss who wouldn't give me a chance, and when I'd come up with an idea of my own, he wanted to give it to someone else. An insatiable ambition that got me in way over my head.

My mom wouldn't have wanted to see me like this. She'd gotten respectable assignments as a journalist. *She'd* covered City Hall and elections, transit strikes, and homelessness. Big stuff. Real stuff.

And to top it all off, I'd had a tryst with my father's top client, whom I'd met before.

The tears finally came, as I knew they would. I put my hand over my mouth in so the cab driver wouldn't hear my sobs.

I cried over my many sorrows. Maybe I had no more than anyone else—but, like everyone else, mine were exquisitely and uniquely agonizing.

I pulled out my phone and scrolled to G. I clicked *Edit* and hesitated for a moment. I scrolled to the *Block this Caller* option and clicked the check box next to it.

There would be no more calls or messages from G, or Varden, or whatever he wanted to be called.

~

Next day at work, I took a swig of the bitter remains of my second cup of coffee. I'd pulled an all-nighter on the Club Silk story, and coffee was the only thing to get me through the day, even though I hated it. I dumped more sugar into it in the hope it might magically become more palatable. It didn't.

I'd sent a draft to Ed. Knowing as eager as he was for it, I figured he was reviewing it at that very moment. So I took the opportunity to draft my letter of resignation. The story on the club was not complete, but there wasn't much more I could do with it. Now it was in Ed's hands, and I'd be sent back to the Garden Club and Little League. And I'd never make enough money to move out of my father's house.

I grabbed my letter off the printer and folded it in thirds, placing it in a long, blank envelope. It was ready for delivery to Ed at the appropriate moment.

Tom appeared at my desk. How the hell had I ever had a crush on such a douchebag? Another one of my lousy decisions.

"Yo, Saff. You running out for Chinese today?" he asked, running his fingers through his hair. The hair I'd once longed to touch, but which I'd now like to set on fire.

I swallowed to keep from exploding. "Don't I go out for the Chinese food every day?"

He recoiled. "Geez, you don't have to get so touchy. It's just that I'm really hungry."

Asshole.

Ed poked his head around the corner and into my cube. "Oh, Tom, didn't know you guys were in a meeting."

Tom jumped to attention. "Oh, hey, boss. We're not meeting. I was just, um, saying hi."

Ed glanced at his watch. "Well, sorry to interrupt you guys, but I gotta be across town for a meeting in thirty minutes. Saffi, do you have a moment to come to my office?"

Without waiting for an answer, he turned to Tom. "And Tom, can you run out and get the Chinese food today?"

Tom stood with his mouth open. I did, too, to be honest. But with Ed quickly retreating into the distance, I grabbed my resignation letter and squeezed out of my cube.

Once inside, I closed his office door behind us.

"Thanks for coming by, Saffi," he said, gesturing toward a chair.

I swallowed hard. Was I going to be fired before I could even resign?

I held my envelope in both hands, picking at one of the corners. Ed had certainly read my draft by now, and I braced myself for the blow that was sure to come.

"So. I read your story."

Would it be bad to just throw the letter at him and leave his office?

Instead, I nodded with my best small but professional smile. "I hope you liked it."

Dream on, girl.

He walked around his desk to perch on its corner. With crossed arms, he looked down and shook his head.

A lump built in my throat and my thoughts jumped ahead to what my next career move might be.

Do not cry in front of the boss. Do. Not. Cry.

"I have to say, your draft blew me away."

Oh god. He hated it.

"It was fantastic."

"Huh?" was all I could manage.

Was he messing with me? Because it sure seemed like it.

"I don't get it."

He threw his head back and laughed. "What's not to get? The work you did was fantastic. Really, really top-notch."

Good thing I was sitting down. I glanced around for a trash can in case I could no longer keep my stomach in check. "Are you serious? You're not joking?"

He was fucking with me. I hated him. Mean, bad man.

"Why the hell would I joke about something like this? The story's great. All it needs is a little tweaking, and we can run it."

The envelope I'd been holding fluttered to the floor. Before I could pick it up, Ed grabbed it.

"This for me?" he asked, seeing his name on the front. He started to open it.

"No!" I snatched it from his hands. "Um, it's something personal. For my *cousin* Ed. I need to mail it later." I crammed it in my back pocket.

"Okay. Let's talk about what needs to be done to finish the story. I really want to get you on to your next assignment."

He blathered on for another fifteen minutes, but to be

honest I only heard about every tenth word. I nodded in agreement and even spat out a few questions that I hoped didn't sound idiotic.

But when I returned to my cube, where my Chinese food was waiting, I knew just what I had to do.

CHAPTER 34

VARDEN

I entered the club, not entirely sure what I was doing there. I guess I just didn't know what else to do.

I looked around the place, which exploded with endless carnal possibilities. The pre-play flirtation had always been a heady aphrodisiac, and I wove through the crowd of beautiful men and women, saying hello and shaking hands until reaching the bar.

"What may I help you with tonight?" The bartender, one I'd never seen before, wiped an invisible spot on the bar.

"Maker's Mark with ginger. And a lime, please."

"Coming right up, sir."

It didn't take long for M to appear at my flank.

"G. Wonderful to see you tonight."

"Hi there." After last time's encounter, it was hard to summon any enthusiasm for the bitch.

"Can we talk?"

I sipped my drink and shrugged. "Sure."

"In my office?" She took my hand.

"Yeah, that's fine."

I'd been to her office once before, a long time ago. It hadn't changed. She closed the door behind us and gestured that I should take the seat next to her.

Instead, I sat in a large wingback chair, crossed a foot over my knee, and leaned back, drink in hand. "What can I help you with, M?"

She looked annoyed I hadn't taken the seat she'd offered.

"G, as you know, I've had some concerns about your friend, B, and her intentions with regard to attending the club."

She ran her fingers through her long, wavy hair.

"She's being banned from the club. I wanted you to know that since you've spent time with her."

"M, I am quite sure she won't be coming back to Club Silk."

"*Really?*"

"She and I...had a disagreement. I wouldn't expect to see her back here."

She filled the room with a loud sigh, and leaned back onto the sofa. "All right then. That takes care of that."

But she continued. "One of the reasons I wanted you to know is that if she tries to return, I can't say she will be safe."

Was she *kidding*?

"Look, M, I know you don't like her, and I'm sure you have your reasons, but what's with the melodrama?"

Unable to help myself, I laughed. "C'mon. She won't be *safe*? You're kidding right?"

Her face hardened, and even in the warm room I felt a chill. She studied me, her expression unchanged, in perfect control as always. "You heard me," she said in a low voice.

I rose from my seat, ready to explode. "You've got to be kidding. Please tell me you are. What is this, the KGB? You're just gonna make people you don't like disappear?"

I was getting louder with every word.

She held her hands up as if to calm me. "I said nothing of the sort."

Bullshit.

"I'm outta here." I pointed a finger at her. "And you're a crazy bitch."

I headed for the door, but before I reached it, she called after me like a dagger in the back.

"G, you know I'm right to protect the club. *Our* club. What would you do without it?"

"Fuck you," I said.

But she'd hit a tender spot. She knew very well how much I depended on the place. Goddammit.

I couldn't get away from her fast enough and beelined from her office straight to the Twist room. I knocked, and the door flew open.

"My man!" said the bouncer, who extended a friendly hand in greeting.

I should have just gone home but couldn't. I just couldn't. I hated that I was so weak, and hated even more that M saw it so clearly.

The bouncer patted me on the back. "You don't look

so happy tonight, my friend. Why don't you just relax and take in the scene? I guarantee it'll cheer you up."

I settled into a corner chair and pulled out my phone.

Shit, shit, shit.

I had to get in touch with Saffi. I scrolled through my contacts and hit *dial*. While waiting for her phone to ring, I watched a woman slide a glass dildo in and out of another. Normally, I'd be all over that shit. But tonight, I had more important things to worry about.

The call rang once and announced the number was not available. It then went directly to a voicemail box that did not contain her greeting.

Wrong number.

I re-dialed. Again, there was one ring, followed by an announcement. The call went to voicemail.

It dawned on me.

She'd blocked my number.

How was I going to get in touch with her, now?

I exited the private room, pushed my way through the crowd, and left the club. Removing my mask, I ran to the car.

CHAPTER 35

SAFFI

I was walking on clouds thanks to Ed's praise, and more determined than ever to get the info I needed to finish my story. The day had clicked by at an agonizing pace, but when it was finally time to head to the club, I couldn't get there fast enough. Ambition. Desire. Secrets. I was learning they were all double-edged swords.

And at the moment, my ambition was a blessing. It kept me from fixating on Varden. But I knew that drama and disappointment would catch up with me later. Things like that always did.

"Hey, Dad," I said, entering his study. "I'm heading out."

He looked up from his computer. "Well, well. I am starting to suspect there is some very lucky young man out there. You look lovely."

I looked down at my trench coat. All that was really showing was my pencil skirt and high heels. He didn't need to see the rest of my outfit.

"Thanks, Dad. I'll see you later."

"Okay, sweetie."

"Oh, Dad?"

"Yeah?" he asked.

"You know that client of yours, Varden? Do you know much about him?"

He set down his pen. "Varden Gallagher? I know a lot about him. Why?"

I shrugged nonchalantly. "I ran into him downtown," I lied.

Dad smiled and his suspicion went right where I thought it would. "He's a ladies' man, Saffi. Set your sights on someone else."

No kidding.

"What else do you know about him?" I asked.

He paused. "Well, he's very successful. Probably one of the richest men in San Francisco. Very hard working and has a lot of integrity. The business he's in does not always attract the most scrupulous people. But from what I've seen of his dealings, he's very trustworthy."

"Huh. Okay." I hadn't expected to hear such high praise. If he only knew...

Confusion crossed his face. "Why are you asking?"

I shrugged with an innocent smile. "I don't know. Just curious, I guess. And nosy."

"All right. Have a great night."

"Thanks, Dad."

On my drive across town, I practiced what I'd say to Miss

M when I arrived. She'd probably be on my ass, asking questions like she usually did. But thanks to Varden's warning, I knew to be careful.

I could just tell her I was working on a story for the Post. What was the harm at this point? If she were smart, she'd cooperate and participate. That way, her perspective would be part of it.

That's what everyone wanted, wasn't it?

I had to admit, in spite of everything else, Varden's warning was a blessing. It was a generous gesture and he'd done me a huge favor. And I sure hadn't thanked him for it. For a moment, I thought about un-blocking him from my phone. I owed him that, didn't I?

I arrived at the club, and before getting out of the car, looked around. From the street, one would never suspect any sign of life beyond the club's heavy wooden door, much less all the sexiness that happened there.

And I knew all M wanted to do was protect that. I couldn't blame her.

I stuffed my trench in the trunk and ran as fast as I could in my heels. As usual, fog billowed down the San Francisco street, leaving me covered in goosebumps by the time I reached the door. For a change, a bouncer opened it. Where was M?

I scanned the room, finding the party in full swing. Couples, threesomes, and small groups sized each other up, enthusiastic about the promise of an erotic encounter.

I figured I'd probably run into Varden—or was it G?— at some point. I needed to level with him, take some responsibility for all that went down. But at the moment, I was here to work.

If M were on to me as Varden had said, it might be my last time in attendance. But for tonight, the plan was to branch out and talk to some different people to see if I could learn anything new. And from the looks of it, it didn't seem it would take long. A man and woman were eying me from the other side of the bar. I nodded back, and they approached.

But before they could reach me, there was a hand on me shoulder.

M.

Big surprise.

"Hi!" I said like I was greeting a long lost friend.

Smiling and elegant beyond description, she placed a hand on my elbow. "So good to see you, my dear. Would you come to my office for a sec to chat?"

"Well, um…" I bobbed my head toward the approaching couple.

But she only tightened her grip. "We won't be long. I'm sure your new friends won't mind." She attempted to steer me in the direction of her office.

I took a look back, and the couple waved to me. I wanted to tell them I'd be right back. Just in case I wasn't. But I didn't get the chance.

We wove through the crowd, dodging everyone who knew M and who wanted to chat. She apologized to them all, saying she had a pressing matter to take care of. The entire time, she never loosened her grip on my elbow.

I steeled myself for a confrontation, thinking through what I might say. Really, there were only two ways to go: deny everything, or admit I was from the paper. Each had its pros and cons.

M ushered me into the office, closing the door behind us. The lock clicked quietly and my awareness jumped into overdrive. I stayed right next to the door, casually leaning against it.

"Please take a seat, B."

I don't think so.

"Thanks M, but I'll stand. I want to get back to my new friends."

She stood close to me. Too close. Somehow, her face remained beautiful while her eyes were dark and hard. "I know you're up to something. I'm not sure what. But I know your type."

I forced a laugh. "That's ridiculous. *My* type. What are you talking about?"

"I want to know what you're doing here. What are you after?"

I kept smiling. "I'm here for the same reason everyone else here is."

I could smell the hatred coming off her. "You don't know me very well, B. But ask anyone. They will tell you I don't suffer fools. And I don't let anyone mess with my club."

"I'm not messing with your club. I don't know what you are talking about." Why hadn't I brought that tiny recorder Ed had offered me?

She moved even closer. Her expensive perfume was exquisite and belied her menacing demeanor. Her fists were balled by her sides.

My heart pounded. It had been a mistake to come here. Especially since I'd told no one where I was. Maybe

Varden was right...being on M's "watch list" could be dangerous.

Before I could think of what to say, there was a loud banging at the door.

M called out, "I'm in a meeting. A *private* meeting."

The banging continued.

"I said I'm in a meeting."

"M, open the goddamn door right now," a familiar voice called through the door. "I know you have B in there with you."

Holy shit, it was Varden. I braced myself against the wall and pushed M as hard as I could. She toppled backward and fell on her ass, her expression one of pure rage.

I turned to flip the lock on the door, and as soon as I did, Varden came flying in. He wasn't wearing his mask. And he was fucking beautiful.

CHAPTER 36

VARDEN

I don't know what I expected to see when I burst into M's office, but it sure as hell wasn't her sprawled on the floor in her expensive silk dress.

I grabbed Saffi's hand and looked her up and down. "Are you okay?"

"Fine. I'm fine," she said.

"You," I said, pointing a finger at M as she reached for a chair to pull herself to her feet, "had better back off."

Standing, she smiled sweetly, smoothing out her dress. "What are you talking about, G? I just invited my friend up here for a little playtime. And she assaulted me."

"Cut the shit." I looked at Saffi and took her hand.

"Wait just a minute," M called after us. "While I don't appreciate being pushed to the ground, to show there are no hard feelings, why don't you take the special room on the third floor? Have it all to yourselves. My treat."

"Thanks, M. Fuck off."

I led Saffi through the crowded club up to the mezzanine and to a secluded corner. The funny thing was that without my mask, no one recognized me. Not a single person said hello.

The irony.

"Jesus. That was close," I said, sinking into a sofa and pulling Saffi down next to me.

"Varden, I just want to tell you—"

But I cut her off.

"Shhh. No need to say anything." She took a deep breath, grasping my hands in her trembling ones.

"Do you really think she was going to do something?" Her face searched mine, which was not surprising. She'd only seen it a couple times.

"I don't know. But I didn't want to find out."

"I'm sorry," she said.

"No, I am."

"Seriously. Thank you, Varden."

"For what?"

"You warned me about her. And then you saved me from her. Thank you."

Her hand was small but strong. I loved her tenacity.

"How did you know I was here?" she asked me.

"It wasn't easy. Did you block me from your phone?"

"Yeah." She shook her head in embarrassment.

"That's what I thought. And I was desperate to get in touch, so I called your dad."

She bolted upright. "You *what*?"

"I called him on the pretense of asking for your number. He gave it to me and also mentioned you'd gone out for the evening all dressed up. It wasn't hard to figure out that you'd come here. I asked for M when I arrived, and they told me she was in her office, not to be disturbed."

I shook my head. "Disturbed my ass. *She's* disturbed."

"Wow," Saffi said quietly. "Just wow. I can't believe the efforts you've made for me, especially after I was such a bitch to you at the Four Seasons."

"I can hardly blame you."

"I also cannot believe you knew me all along, and on top of that, are my father's client." She slapped my thigh. It was the least I deserved.

"I know, I know. I'd planned on eventually telling you. I just hadn't figured out when. At first it was a little game, and then..."

She looked at me. "And then what?"

I watched the crowd filing by. "I don't know. I found myself thinking of you. You know, I wasn't lying when I told you how beautiful you are. But I also respect how driven you are. I see some of myself in you."

She gave me a sexy smile. "I think that's not the only area where we are compatible."

Booyah.

She leaned to press her lips against mine, parting them to steal a small taste. I followed her lead until I could wait no longer, and then drew her to me with a hand on the back of her head. My lips ground against hers until we could barely breathe. I wanted to inhale her, all of her, so I'd never forget what she smelled and tasted like.

A couple interrupted, addressing Saffi. "Hey, we're wondering if you'd like to get a drink with us," the man said.

"Thanks. But I'm gonna hang out with my friend here tonight," she answered.

They smiled and moved on. Thatta girl.

"Their loss, my gain, B. Also known as Saffi," I said.

"I'm right where I want to be. Speaking of which..."

She hiked her skirt up to her thighs and straddled my lap and ran light kisses from my temple to my jaw and back to my lips. In the confines of my trousers, my cock ached. Nothing new, there.

I wanted to take her. But not yet.

Sneaking a hand under the hem of her blouse, my fingers wandered over her heated flesh until I found her perfect tits. With a circular motion, I rubbed her hard points with my open palms. My fingers gradually closed over them, and her soft sighs whispered against my mouth.

"Stand up, baby," I said in her ear. She backed off my lap.

I rose, too, and took her face in my hands. "You know what I want to do to you, right?"

She bit the corner of her lip.

"I have no idea," she said in a coy voice.

Goddamn, she was sweet.

"Well darlin', I think I might just need to fuck you." She shuddered and leaned next to my ear.

"You want some pussy, mister?"

Jesus Christ.

I spun her to face the sofa and hiked up her pencil skirt until her thigh-high stockings and tiny lace thong were in full view of anyone walking by. What a vision, with those fuck me shoes and creamy round ass.

Pushing her to kneel on the sofa, I pressed her head to rest against its back. Bent at an almost-ninety degree angle, her exposed ass caught the attention of several passersby. She shimmied just enough to draw approving murmurs from the growing audience.

I crouched behind her and ran my tongue along the narrow strip of fabric covering her pussy and asshole. She wiggled and then whined when I backed off, leaving her wanting.

When she was still, I went in for more. Again, her she wiggled her ass with a demanding groan. I stood and bent close to her ear. "You like my tongue in your crack, baby? Nod if you do."

Her head bobbed wildly, spilling her long hair onto the sofa back.

With a tight fist, I grabbed her thong panty and yanked it. The tension split the fabric at the seams, and I tossed it to the floor. Now she was totally uncovered, her glistening, bare pussy and tight, pink asshole.

I got back to work, my tongue sliding from the top of her crack to her opening, where I buried my tongue deep in her wet folds. She writhed as her juices spilled onto my face, and they tasted damn good.

We were finally where I wanted us to be and my aim was to drive her crazy. I spread her wetness with my tongue, getting her ready for my hard cock.

Unable to wait any longer, I pulled my erection out of my pants and began stroking it. I drove one finger, and then two inside her, leaving her bucking like a wild woman. Her pussy clenched around my fingers, and she screamed my name as her first orgasm washed over her. It wasn't going to be her last.

I left my crouch to line my cock up with her, grabbing a condom from my pocket. She clearly liked being watched and pretty soon, she was going to like being fucked.

I reached around for her hard clit, and leaned toward her ear again. "You ready for me to fuck you, beautiful?"

All she could manage was a nod and some sort of squeak.

"All right," I whispered. "Baby's gonna get some cock."

I dragged my cock up and down her to get it wet, and bounced the crown over her pussy until she wiggled in agony. But instead of giving it to her, I had another idea.

I took my thumb and dipped it deep into her creamy opening. When it was good and wet, I ran it up to her asshole, pressing gently against the tight opening. She jumped and then pushed back on my finger for more.

At the same time, I positioned my cock at her soaked pussy and pushed an inch or two into her tight heat, waiting for her to accommodate more of me. I reveled in the little tremors pulsing around my dick—she squeezed so tightly, I nearly blew my load.

With my cock in her pussy and thumb invading her ass, she arched to take me more deeply. Over the din of the club, her moans reverberated.

The more excited she got, the harder she pushed back against me. I finally dove deep inside her pussy, pistoning in and out while she cried for more. Her entire body began to shudder, and I fucked her harder, wanting to feel her come again. Her pussy clenched in spasms, and I joined her, burying my cock balls-deep and thrusting the full length of my thumb in her ass.

Her reaction, mixed with the joy on the faces of the onlookers, was intoxicating. I continued to pump, spurting into her, until my shaking legs forced me to stop. I eased out and collapsed, grabbing her around the waist and dragging her on top of me on the sofa.

The audience wandered away while we held each other and caught our breaths. M leaned against the wall, watching us. When I caught her eye, she turned on her heel and disappeared into the crowd.

Bye, bitch.

CHAPTER 37

SAFFI

H oly shit.

I'd never come like that before, and even though I was safe in Varden's arms, my trembling continued.

Safe. That's what it was. I wasn't sure I'd ever felt so safe.

"Oh my god," I mumbled.

"Jesus. That was freaking hot."

"Varden?"

"Yes, baby?"

"What are we gonna tell my dad? You asked him for my number, so he obviously knows something's up."

"If it's okay with you, I'd like to talk to him alone."

"Well, I don't usually let other people do my speaking for me. But in this case, I guess it might be okay. Would you be nervous?"

"Not sure I'd say nervous. I mean, I've done a lot of

business with your dad. I know he thinks well of me. But he knows I haven't had the best reputation with the ladies. He might not want me coming anywhere near you."

He had a point.

I squeezed his hand. "I think if we're honest, he'll be okay. He knows I'm not an idiot."

He looked at me. "Come home with me tonight. I'll drive you back to your dad's in the morning."

My heart leapt.

"Let's go."

We headed toward the door of the club, earning a few admiring nods on the way. And yet, without his mask, no one knew who Varden was.

Once we arrived in Varden's amazing penthouse apartment, he hollered, "Beau! I got a friend with me."

A man emerged from the back who, with his dark eyes and chiseled face, could have been his twin. But Varden was a smidge taller and definitely more buff. I extended my hand.

"So you're the one?" Beau asked.

His smile rivaled his brother's. Good lord. I couldn't believe there were two of them.

I looked at Varden. "You talked about me?"

"I might have." He turned to Beau. "Thanks for outing me, bro."

"Oh shit, didn't mean to cause any trouble," he said, laughing. "And…I think I'll excuse myself now."

He disappeared into his room.

"Wow," Saffi said. "Your brother could give you a run for your money."

Varden grabbed me by the waist and pulled me to him.

"You're right. He's a great guy. Had some challenges, but he's making it work. I help him all I can."

"He's lucky to have you."

Varden nodded. "I'm the lucky one. In more ways than one."

Next morning, Varden found me wearing the fluffy white bathrobe I'd helped myself to. I was watching the San Francisco sunrise from his vast windows and he walked up behind me and wrapped his arms tightly around me.

"This view is insane," I said.

He turned me to face him and stepped back to look me up and down. "I have to say, that robe has never looked better."

"Oh, you say that to all the girls."

"Actually...I've never had a girl spend the night here before. You're the first to wrap that robe around your hot, little body."

And right there, in front of the floor-to-ceiling windows, he started to unwrap me, his hands inching toward my breasts.

"Wait! Your brother."

"Oh shit. Almost forgot about little Beau." He took my hand and led me back to the bedroom.

Once inside, he yanked the robe from me, dropping it to the floor. Under his Egyptian cotton pajama bottoms, his now-erect cock screamed for attention. He pushed them to his ankles and engulfed his bouncing erection in his huge hand, stroking it from base to bulging head.

It was the first time I'd seen him fully naked, and he was glorious. Whenever we'd played at the club, he'd always been partially clothed.

This had definitely been worth waiting for.

His broad shoulders and upper arms bulged with the curve of muscle, and the inside of one forearm was tattooed with a clock. His nipples were erect and brown, surrounded by a perfect splay of chest hair that vee'd into a long, thin line past his belly button to where his hand rested on his cock.

Without the robe, I, too, was completely exposed and thanks to his admiring gaze, I'd never felt as beautiful.

"Kneel." He motioned toward the long, upholstered bench in front of another expansive window.

I padded over and settled on my knees. "Like this?" I asked.

"Yeah." He walked up behind me, directing me to bend all the way down until my cheek rested on the cushion. He hoisted my hips as high as they would go and spread my knees. From my position, I watched him step back and look at me on full display. I felt his gaze wander from my ass past my pussy, to the top of my slit where my clit was peeking out.

"Fuck, yeah," he growled.

"Someone might see us," I said, peeking out the window.

"I thought you'd like that."

He was right.

My hand wandered back between my legs and one finger landed on the erect bud of my clit. Varden groaned.

"What a sight," he murmured, reaching into his dresser.

He stretched a condom over his length and ran his tongue from my ass all the way through my lips and back up.

"Damn, you taste good," he told me, leaving me shivering beneath him.

"You like licking my pussy and ass? Maybe you can lick it again? Please?" I begged.

He straddled the bench just behind me so my ass was perfectly in line with his face. He licked a finger and circled it around my tight opening. As he loosened me, I moaned and pushed back on his finger.

"You like it in your ass, don't you?"

"Mmmm. I've never had it in my ass," I murmured. "Except for your finger."

He pushed in farther. "Yeah? Tell me if it's too much."

I wiggled my ass in the air. "More. I want more." I trusted him to do anything he wanted.

He introduced a second finger and gently pushed until I relaxed. With two fingertips inside, he pumped them in and out until they were buried to his knuckles.

Electricity shot from my core to every nerve ending. I'd never dreamed ass play would leave me trembling like this.

"You good?" he asked.

"Mmmm." I moved my hips to meet his thrusts, and soon, his fingers were completely buried. He gradually increased the speed of his pistoning until I pounded my fists on the bench and began to moan.

"Give it to me. I want more. Fuck me, Varden. I want your cock in there," I begged.

If I didn't get it I might lose my mind.

"You sure, baby?"

"Please...please," I murmured.

I twisted around to see him reach for some lube. He coated himself with it and drizzled some down my crack, making me jump and the tickling sensation. I waved my ass in the air like a dog in heat.

A different pressure bounced against my ass, much larger than Varden's fingers. I rubbed my clit, focused on relaxing my tight ring of muscle.

He pressed against my opening, his tip stretching me and gradually dipping past my rim. When the widest part of his head passed through, I jumped at the slight burn. I exhaled, and he glided in more easily. He sank deeper into me and I jammed myself back on him. He reached forward and held my head down. A thousand tiny explosions racked my body with a sensation I'd never known existed.

I loved it.

My moans rose to a crescendo and I continued rocking my hips against him.

"God, Varden. I love it," I murmured over and over again.

He pumped harder, his balls bouncing against my pussy. I reached back and thrust two fingers in myself and to feel his dick on the other side of my wall.

"You love what, baby?" he teased.

"Your cock in my ass. Fuck me, fuck my ass," I cried as my body shook in violent shudders. My orgasm hit so hard, I started to slide off the bench.

But he righted me just in time, like I knew he would. I twisted my head free of his grasp, my orgasm continuing to roll from the sensitive nerves of my ass to my fingers, toes, and scalp, in wave after wave of inconceivable ecstasy.

Behind me, he groaned. With one last thrust, he buried himself as deeply as he ever had in my pulsating ass, and with a tight grip on my hips, delivered his load. When he was done, he pulled out gradually, scooping me up in his arms and carrying me to the bed.

Curling up on my side, I was beyond spent. Varden pulled me toward him in a tight spoon, and everything went dark.

CHAPTER 38

VARDEN

Thank god it was Saturday morning.

After an incredible session in front of the window, my girl had completely passed out. I was in need of some recovery time, too. She was so beautiful as she dozed, vulnerable yet strong.

And the enthusiastic way she let me pop her ass cherry —well, that would give me something to jerk off to for years to come.

I had to figure out how to break the news of our relationship to Saffi's dad. Hugh Bartlett knew me as a hard-driving professional as well as a man-whore when off the clock. He might not want his daughter to have anything to do with me.

Couldn't blame him, really.

Saffi stirred, looking around my room as if she didn't know where she was. "Wow. What time is it?"

"Ten a.m."

"Oh my god! My dad's gonna think I'm dead in a ditch. Why didn't I text him last night? Shit."

She jumped out of bed and scrambled for her cell. "He'll be so worried."

"He should be," Varden said.

She whipped her head around. "Why?"

He ran his fingers through his bed head. "I'm sure it's no surprise to you that I haven't exactly been the settling down type—"

"And my dad is aware of that?"

He nodded slowly. "Everyone's aware of that."

She lowered herself to the bench where all the fun had happened the night before. "So what am I doing here?"

I looked up at the bedroom ceiling, then gazed directly at her. "Everything is different with you. I want you in my life. You're amazing, smart, beautiful, sexy, kind—"

"Oh my god." Her eyes filled with tears and her chin quivered. "Thank you. I mean, not thank you, but that's so kind. No, not kind, that's not what I meant—"

I pressed my fingers to her lips. "Shhh. You don't have to say anything."

She sniffled and cleared her throat. "There are two calls from my dad." She played the first one.

"Saffi, hey there, just checking in. I don't mind your spending the night out, but I'd really like you to let me know when you're not coming home. Talk to you soon, sweetie."

I winced. Damn.

"I'll text him that I'm on my way home. Can you give me a lift to my car? I left it at the club."

"Of course. In fact, I think I'll follow you to your dad's. We'll all have a talk."

"Sure you want to do that?" she asked me with a raised brow.

"Hey, I gotta start showing I'm a new man some time, don't I?"

She ran around the room, gathering her clothes from the night before. Could I really move from being mister man-whore to smitten with the beautiful Saffi?

"There's one thing I wanted to ask you about," I said. "Have you given any thought to exactly, um...who might show up in your story for the Post?"

She cupped the sides of my face. "You are *not* going to be in the story. Do you think I want everyone to know that during my undercover investigation I, um, tested the merchandise?"

Grabbing her hand, we headed for my car.

Driving separately, we pulled up before her father's massive house in one of the city's upscale neighborhoods. It was vastly different from the downtown high rise where I lived, and yet the advantages of having more space, and peace and quiet, were obvious. I'd never been to Hugh's home and was glad to see the man rewarded himself for being available to clients like me nearly twenty-four seven.

He deserved to live well.

Saffi waited on the front step for me to park, and then

let us into the house. The entryway was vast and beautifully decorated.

"Wow," I whispered, looking around, "you grew up here?"

She nodded. "I did. My mom decorated the place. She had a real talent for that sort of thing."

"Man, you should see where Beau and I grew up."

"Really?"

"Yeah. Just a *little* different from this place." I pictured the shitty little trailer Beau and I had called home. I was also quite sure Saffi hadn't worried about being smacked around by drunks during her childhood.

"Dad?" she called.

"Hi, sweetie. In here." Hugh's voice rang from the other side of the house.

We walked into a darkly paneled study with comfortable, crackled, broken-in leather furniture. The room smelled of cognac and a slight mustiness, most likely from the hundreds of books lining the walls.

"Varden," Hugh said with surprise when he saw me follow Saffi in.

"Hugh. How are you?" I crossed the room to shake hands.

He stood and automatically extended his hand, but the look on his face was confused.

"I didn't expect to see you two here. Together. What a surprise." He looked back and forth between us.

Damn, he was diplomatic. No wonder he was a top attorney.

"Dad, I want to explain—"

But I interrupted. "No, Saffi. Let me explain, please.

Mind if we sit, Hugh?" I gestured to the chairs opposite the desk. I had to speak fast. I knew how Saffi felt about being spoken for.

"Please. Be my guests."

Saffi looked at me with wide eyes.

I cleared my throat. "Hugh, Saffi and I have seen each other socially a few times, and have decided to start dating."

I reached for Saffi's hand. "I hope that's okay with you, and I hope it doesn't burden our working relationship."

Hugh rubbed his chin and tilted his head back to look at the ceiling. Shit, maybe this wouldn't go as well as I'd hoped.

But he took a deep breath. "Were you at Varden's last night?" he asked Saffi.

She looked directly back at him. "Yes, Dad. I stayed over his place." God, she was gutsy.

He looked over at me.

"Varden, you know Saffi's my precious girl." He looked down at his hands.

"I've always dreamt that she'd find the kind of happiness her mother and I had. Now, I know you guys say you are just starting to date. But if I could choose an upstanding man for my daughter"—he looked back up—"I would choose you."

He broke into a huge smile.

Saffi and I looked at each other in disbelief. My beautiful girl was beaming.

"Saffi," Hugh said, motioning toward me, "this man is one of the most ethical and upstanding clients I've ever had. I completely trust him."

Holy shit. I'd hoped he thought well of me, but I hadn't expected praise like that. My own eyes welled up at the kindest thing anyone had ever said about me.

Saffi jumped up from her chair, kissed my cheek, and and ran to hug her father. "Thank you for trusting us, Dad. I was concerned there might be some...difficulty."

"You're a grown woman. You can do what you want. But I am honored you both came to me."

I stood and extended my hand again.

"Hugh," I said, my voice cracking. "I appreciate the vote of confidence."

I looked at Saffi.

"We both appreciate it."

CHAPTER 39 & OTHER STUFF

SAFFI

Three weeks later, I moved all the crap from my cubicle to my very own office, where the paper's new receptionist dropped off the Chinese food I'd ordered for lunch. The sign hanging on the door said *Saffi Bartlett* nice and big.

"I really appreciate your running out for us," I told the new girl. "I used to get the Chinese food myself, and it got really old after awhile."

The receptionist smiled shyly. "My pleasure, Saffi. I can't complain. I'm just so happy to be here at the paper. Maybe we could have coffee sometime and you could tell me about how you moved up through the ranks?"

"I'd love that. Let's do it."

Wait till she heard my story. Or didn't.

At that afternoon's staff meeting, Ed was at the head of the conference room, like usual. When everyone finally filed in, his hands went up to quiet the room. "We have a lot to go over today, gang. But what I think is most exciting is that Saffi's story about Club Silk has been nominated for the Investigative Reporting Annual Award."

I looked around the room. Everyone was staring back at me.

Wait. What did he just say?

My coworkers were clapping and cheering.

I guess I'd heard him right.

I clutched my hand to my chest. "Oh my gosh. Thank you, guys. Thank you, Ed."

"Well, you deserve it, Saffi. You were courageous and did a great job."

Even Tom, with an eye on the cute receptionist, seemed happy for me.

Another thing to talk to her about over lunch...

The office hadn't been my only move. I arrived home that night and threw my keys on the penthouse's kitchen counter. I still had some boxes to unpack from my dad's house, but was getting settled in nicely.

"Varden?" I called.

"In here, babe."

I followed his voice to find him in the den. He was throwing items in a large green garbage bag.

"Whatcha doin'?"

He held up his mask from Club Silk. "Thinking it's time to say goodbye to this baby." He tossed it in the bag.

"Wait! You could always save it, put it on a shelf or something."

He considered it for a moment. "You know, I don't want it. I'm not hiding anymore."

"Are you sure?"

He placed his hands on either side of my face. "Hiding is my past. Loving you is my future." He planted his mouth on mine for a knee-wobbling, breathtaking kiss.

That all-too-familiar throb between my legs began to make itself known. There'd been a lot of that since I'd moved into the penthouse.

"And Beau is okay with everything?"

"He's more than okay. He's thrilled. He thinks the world of you. And he seems to like his new place. I think he's really turned things around."

Tears sprung to my eyes.

"How did I get lucky enough to fall into the Gallagher family?"

He smiled. "How did I get lucky enough to fall into the Bartlett family?"

Easing me against the game table, he pulled my dress over my head. I unhooked my bra and let it fall to the floor and his hands flew to my bare breasts as kisses sprinkled over my hard nipples. He took one between his teeth and gently tugged.

My head spun with desire. This man knew exactly how to touch me every moment of every day.

How did he do that, find the connection that drew us together over and over again, that left me so weak in the knees?

"We could head over to the club if you want to. But things seem pretty hot right here."

He wasn't kidding.

"Oh, wait a sec." I relayed the story of my award.

"God, baby, I'm so proud of you. You killed it, just like I knew you would."

"Couldn't have done it without you, you know. *And* we salvaged our relationship with M."

"Oh yeah." He turned me around and slid my panties down to run his tongue along my aching pussy.

"And I'll be forever in your debt for not outing me as a club member," he added with a laugh.

I moaned as my clit throbbed with heaviness. "I like your being in my debt." I turned to face him, licking my taste from his lips and tongue.

"You could have broken me," he said.

"I'd say I did break you. And then I put you back together."

He lay me back on the game table, sending chess pieces flying to the floor.

"You're right. I'm happier, stronger, wiser, and…more complete. I've found all I need," he told me.

I nodded in agreement. And there would always be more stories to write, and maybe even awards to win. But until then, we had each other. And together, we were more than enough.

Get a FREE steamy short story!
Join my Insider Group

If you liked *Dirty Little Secret*, check out this excerpt from:

Sinful Little Betrayal

Chapter 1
Nara

"You are *not* my husband, Simon. Stop telling people that."

"Nara my dear, but I *am* your husband. And I will tell anyone I please that I'm your husband."

Good thing he was on the other end of the phone line.

I swallowed hard. I couldn't let him know how he rattled me. "I don't know why you are making this so hard. We agreed that as soon as you got your US citizenship, we'd start on the divorce." I lowered my voice so the whole office didn't hear.

Long sigh, followed by a chuckle.

Smug fuck.

"Darling. Darling. Now, you *know* what you have to do if you want to cast me off so badly. 'Course that one night in London…well, it didn't seem like you wanted to ever leave my side. Or should I say, my *cock*?"

God. The mistake of a lifetime. We'd been in London, his hometown, taking fake pictures to prepare for our big, fake US Immigration and Naturalization Service interview where we were going to fake being in love. Simon had hired a friend to drive us to several different locations —with wardrobe changes—to take photos that would show how in love we were and that we would never, ever try to fool the INS. People did it all the time he'd assured me, and there was ten thousand dollars in it for me. Good news all around.

Except for the one night I drank too much and ended up in bed with said future faux husband.

That had not been part of the deal. While he had that awesome British accent that Americans love, he also had bad teeth, a pasty complexion, and was at least two inches shorter than I. And yet, I'd fucked him.

Oh, to do things over. But I'd needed that money. I'd been working on developing my software app for three long years with little income. Crashing on my best friend's couch was getting old. Really old. That's when I answered a Craigslist ad to marry someone for a green card. It had sounded easy at the time, just like that adorable 90's movie *Green Card*, I told myself. And now I was stuck with the bastard.

"Simon," I said with all the fake patience I could muster, "that was a fun night. It really was." I choked on the biggest lie I'd ever told. Truth was, I remembered nothing of our tryst, and that was just fine with me.

But I could hear him smiling through the phone. How I wished I could smack that grin off his face.

I continued, "But sweetie…"

I could almost hear him puffing his chest out.

"We've taken care of business. We both got what we wanted. I'm grateful for that. And now, it's time to honor the last piece of our agreement." How could he argue with that?

"I'll tell you what," he said as if he hadn't heard a word I'd just said. "My latest offer still stands. If you repay me the ten grand, I'll disappear out of your life forever. We'll annul the marriage and go on about our business like it never happened."

My face burned, and my hands shook. "Look. I helped you get your green card. You're in. You're as good as American, thanks to me. I earned that ten grand, I lied for you, married you, and even fucked you—"

"That was only one time—"

"*That's not the point.* You need to forget about extorting money from me. Give it up. It's not gonna happen. Plus, I don't have ten grand to give you even if I wanted to." A migraine circled my head like a bird looking for a place to land. *Not now*, I begged. I needed my wits about me.

"Oh, Nara. We all know your software company has grown nicely. I'm sure you could write a check right now and be done with it," he said.

Where did he get such a stupid assumption? I'd been breaking my back over my Mommy Knows for years. Yes, we were starting to get a little press. Yes, we were attracting the eye of potential customers and investors. But that didn't mean I had two nickels to rub together. We were waiting for investors to come through, and until they did, the company was surviving off a line of credit. And getting perilously close to maxing that out. If we didn't get an infusion of cash soon, I had no idea what I'd do.

"Let me make this very clear," he said. "If you do not come up with the money I'm asking for, I will make sure all your current and future investors know you committed the felony of defrauding the INS. That will speak volumes about your character, and no one will touch your company with a ten-foot pole. And, I will not make it easy to divorce me."

He paused for effect. "So, darling, what will it be?"

The migraine was no longer circling. It had landed with a crash, feasting on my poor little brain. Eyes closed, I rummaged through my desk for a pill, the only thing that would save my day. But it's hard to find things with closed eyes. A loose pile of staples stabbed my thumb.

I said slowly and steadily, "I do not have ten thousand dollars. And if you ruin my company or me, there is even less chance that I ever will. You know that. You'd be sabotaging yourself."

It seemed he was thinking, due to the momentary silence.

"I want that money. I'll give you a month. I don't care how you get it. Take a cash advance on one of your credit cards, for god's sake."

Could I have hated someone more at that moment?

A movement caught my eye, and I turned toward the opening of my office-that-was-really-a-cubicle.

Joi—my best friend, my founding partner, my chief financial officer—stood in the doorway. I loved having her in charge of the money. She wasn't getting paid much, either, so she spent most of her days chasing after investors so that she someday would. I held up a *wait a minute* finger and turned back to my call.

"Simon, I have a meeting I have to run to. We'll continue this conversation later."

"I wouldn't wait too long—"

I hung up on the asshole.

No, I could never have hated someone more.

<u>Read more of Nara's story...</u>

Get a free short story!
<u>Join my Insider Group</u>

ALSO BY MIKA LANE

The Anti-Hero Chronicles
Dirty Game / Audio
Nasty Bet / Audio
Filthy Deal / Audio
Foolish Dare / Audio

**The Savage Mountain
Men Reverse Harem Series**
The Captive / Audio
The Runaway / Audio
The Pursued / Audio
The Prize / Audio
Boxset books 1-4 / Audio

Contemporary Reverse Harem
The Inheritance / Audio
The Renovation / Audio
The Promotion / Audio
The Gallery / Audio
The Collection / Audio

Boxset books 1-5

A Player Romance series 1-3
Mister Hollywood
Mister Fake Date
Mister Wrong

Billionaire Duet 1-2
Dirty Little Secret
Sinful Little Betrayal

STAY IN THE KNOW
Join my Insider Group
Exclusive access to private release specials, giveaways, the opportunity to receive advance reader copies (ARCs), and other random musings.

LET'S KEEP IN TOUCH
Mika Lane Newsletter
Email me
Visit me! www.mikalane.com
Friend me! Facebook
Pin me! Pinterest
Follow me! Twitter
Laugh with me! Instagram

ABOUT THE AUTHOR

Dear Reader:

Please join my Insider Group and be the first to hear about giveaways, sales, pre-orders, ARCs, and other cool stuff: http://mikalane.com/join-mailing-list.

Writing has been a passion of mine since, well, forever (my first book was "The Day I Ate the Milkyway," a true fourth-grade masterpiece). These days, steamy romance, both dark and funny, gives purpose to my days and nights as I create worlds and characters who defy the imagination. I live in magical Northern California with my own handsome alpha dude, sometimes known as Mr. Mika Lane, and an evil cat named Bill. These two males also defy my imagination from time to time.

A lover of shiny things, I've been known to try to new recipes on unsuspecting friends, find hiding places so I can read undisturbed, and spend my last dollar on a plane ticket somewhere.

I have several titles for you to choose from including the perennially favorite Billionaire and Reverse Harem stories. And have you see my Player Series about male escorts who make the ladies of Hollywood curl their toes and forget their names? Hottttt.... And my brand new anti-hero/mafia books are coming out in audio as I write this.

Exciting news: in June 2020, I will be publishing with Vi Keeland's and Penelope Ward's Cocky Hero Club as one of their contributing authors. Stay tuned for more on this or follow my Facebook page: https://www.facebook.com/mikalaneauthor. And, as if that's not cool enough, I am also writing in K. Bromberg's Everyday Heroes world. Look for that later in the year.

I'll always promise you a hot, sexy romp with kick-ass but imperfect heroines, and some version of a modern-day happily ever after.

I LOVE to hear from readers when I'm not dreaming up naughty tales to share. Join my Insider Group so we can get to know each other better http://mikalane.com/join-mailing-list, or contact me here: https://mikalane.com/contact.

xoxo
    Love,
    Mika